CW00662998

Cover Design and Interior format by The Killion Group
http://thekilliongroupinc.com

KEIRA
MONTCLAIR

Patrol Team

Connor Grant — Sela Grant

Derric Corbett — **Dyna Corbett**

Ethan Matheson — Jennet Matheson

Isla Matheson

Marcas Matheson — Brigid Matheson

Reyna Matheson

Gavin Ramsay — Merewen Ramsay

Ysenda Ramsay

Cailean MacAdam — Sorcha MacAdam

Cadyn MacAdam
Ceit MacAdam

Donnan Douglas — Bethia Douglas

Thea Douglas

Drew Menzie — Avelina Menzie

Maitland Menzie

Torcall Massie — Riley Massie

Tevis Massie

Jamie Grant — Gracie Grant

Alaric Grant

Lucas Grant — Iva Grant

Dobbin Grant

Geoffrey MacGriffin

Lewis MacMahon

PROLOGUE

From the Epilogue of The Scot's Traitor—
a reminder of the situation for Wulf and Reyna...

A HORSE APPEARED ACROSS the meadow, flying directly toward them. One who was just arriving on Ramsay land, two other horses now joining the lead horse.

Reyna frowned. "Oh, I dinnae like this."

"Who is it?" Wulf asked.

"Dyna. The other leader of the patrol. If she's coming it means something has happened. Ceit and Alaric are behind her."

"I knew it."

"What?" Reyna asked.

His gut dropped because he knew what Dyna would say. Something had happened, and it had to do with Tryana.

He should have killed his father when he had the chance.

Dyna approached, stopping her horse directly in front of them, her breathing slowing so she could catch her breath. Ceit and Alaric stopped behind her.

"'Tis Tryana." He stated what he knew the truth was, without a doubt.

Dyna nodded. "I had a dream about her, so we traveled to the abbey the next morn."

"And?" he asked impatiently, his heart thudding in his chest.

"Tryana and Cadyn are both gone. They left in the middle of the night…"

and the story continues…

CHAPTER ONE

Late summer, 1315, England

Cadyn MacAdam of Clan Ramsay brushed his horse down in the stable at Ellonton Abbey in North Yorkshire. He'd volunteered to protect a lass whose sire had betrothed her to a bastard, and he vowed to keep his word. As a Ramsay guard, this was his first assignment where he was alone, and he could not fail.

The sound of hoofbeats caught him—more than one horse—so he stepped out to see who it could be. Four horses headed their way but he couldn't tell who the riders were yet. A squeal from inside the curtain wall of the abbey forced him to toss his brush to the stable boy and head inside the gate.

"Cadyn, Cadyn! Where are you?"

He made it inside just in time to catch Tryana de Gray as she launched herself at him. He held her close and whispered, "What has ye so upset?"

"'Tis the baron. I saw him out the window. I recognized him." She paused to catch her breath. "Please don't let him take me away."

Tryana, all soft curves and warmth, melded her body against him, and he had to force himself to do the honorable thing. "Dinnae worry. I will protect ye. The man canno' forcibly remove ye from an abbey, lass. Ye must remember that."

He set her back and her eyes misted as she stared up at him. "I pray you are right. Will you tell him? Please?"

"I will greet him. Ye go back inside and I'll take care of it. I'd prefer it if ye were in the abbey where he canno' see ye." He brushed the strands of hair back from his face. "Go now." It was just past high sun so the man was trying to do it the right way instead of attacking in the middle of the night. That was a small consolation.

She nodded and spun on her boot heel to hurry back inside. Fortunately, she believed most everything he told her.

Cadyn made his way to the large oak tree in front of the abbey, taking his bow with him. He loved both his bow and his sword, but the English preferred their small swords, so he'd take the four on with his bow. Best weapon for the situation.

The four horses arrived at the gate of the abbey. Most times they were left open so anyone could come to pray, but with Tryana in residence, they'd been kept closed. "State yer business," said the guard.

"I've come for my betrothed. I am the Baron of Topcliffe, Gareth Ward."

The guard replied, "She's choosing to remain in the abbey, my lord."

"I do not care what she wants. I have proof of the betrothal. You will return her to me."

Cadyn nocked his arrow from the branch he was braced on, then let it fly over the men's heads as a warning. "She'll be staying. Take yer leave before I fire lower."

The baron's head ducked, but the fury was evident in his face. His voice came out in a snarl. "Who are you?"

"Cadyn MacAdam of Clan Ramsay, assigned as Tryana's protector. Ye will leave now or I have another four arrows, one for each of ye. I'll start with legs and arms." He fired another one wild, but close enough to spook the front horse.

"My lord?" This came from the poor guard trying to settle his spooked horse.

The baron shouted at him. "We will leave, but this is not over. Expect us to return with a writ from the king and more guards." They turned their mounts around and left.

He waited until they were far enough away, glad at how that had played out. This was his first assignment by himself, and he could not, would not fail. More important than anything, he wished to be known as one of the best Ramsay guards and he had many reasons.

To make his parents and grandparents proud of him.

To make his clan chieftain proud.

And to be invited to be a spy for the Scottish Crown, just as his grandsire had been in his younger days. This was his main goal in life, and he would do whatever he could to see it come to fruition.

Once they were out of sight, he hopped down from the tree and stepped inside the gate. He strode in through the front door of the abbey just in time to see Tryana flying down the nearby staircase and hugging him swiftly.

Hell, but it surely felt fine to have this beautiful woman in his arms, all soft and sweet.

"Many thanks to you, Cadyn. Do you think they'll return?" She looked at him with such admiration that it humbled him. Being the hero was agreeing with him. This gave him the time to notice how pretty she was, her dark brown hair holding streaks of gold in it. Her eyes were the same blue as Wulf's, an unusual color for dark-haired people. The blue eyes made her stunning, her high cheekbones giving her the look of a princess, though she'd never believe it.

"Dinnae worry if they do. I'll protect ye, Tryana. Please excuse me for now. I must return to the stables to refill my quiver."

He didn't wish to tell her the truth. He was going to make sure they didn't return.

Tryana de Gray was in the middle of the toughest battle she'd ever endured, one that made her wish, more than anything, that her mother was still here. An overwhelming cloud of impending doom threatened her but she refused to give in to it. This battle was not over, the battle of inner wills, of a woman's right to have a say in her future, this battle with two men who intended to control her until the day she died.

She wouldn't have it.

The time had come, not something she'd looked forward to, but something she knew would come one day. It was time for Tryana de Gray to stand up for herself, to become strong enough to repel two men she hated more than any other: her father and her betrothed.

Her mother was dead and had been for many years, her brother was happily in love with Reyna Matheson, so it was up to her to find a way to free herself of the two men who were bound to chase her down, follow her, and try to steal her away. From her seat in the small chamber inside Ellonton Abbey, she thought about the battle she faced and forced herself to be brave. Defying her father and breaking her betrothal were terrifying to her, but she had no other choice.

Wulf, her only brother, had managed to find her at her betrothed's manor home. Though Wulf had been captured and imprisoned by English soldiers before he could rescue her, he had arranged for Reyna to steal her away from the baron's noble torture chamber. Reyna's Scottish companions had brought her to the abbey, a safe haven from her father and her betrothed, the baron.

But was it a safe haven?

A normal Englishman would accept whatever the abbess told him, would walk away from the abbey after being turned away at the gates. But neither her father nor the baron were the type of men to take no for an answer. And neither one of them liked to be told what to do by a woman, not even an abbess.

Tryana and her protector, Cadyn, had been here for two days, but with each passing hour, she could feel the dread growing inside her, a feeling that she recognized as being brewed from the proximity of either her sire, Wrath de Gray, or her betrothed, Gareth Ward. And now that the baron had attempted to retrieve her, she couldn't help but wonder what would be bubbling up next.

She had known one of them was close. Too close. Just hearing the baron's voice from her window had made her hair stand on end. He was a cruel man.

A few hours had passed since then, so she returned the Bible she'd been reading to a safe place, hiding it under her pillow, then made her way out of the small bedchamber and down the passageway to the staircase to the inner courtyard, hoping to find Cadyn there. Dusk was nigh upon them and they needed to talk now.

The passage was lit by flickering torches placed every few feet along the walls in the abbey. The stone was cold and worn smooth, but she watched her footing to avoid tripping on the uneven floor as she crept toward the staircase. She was utterly petrified, fearing that one of those horrid men would jump out from the shadows and take her prisoner. She held her breath in trepidation.

Tryana tiptoed quietly down the back stairs until she found the bottom, then peeked across the main passageway toward the primary entrance to the abbey. Seeing nothing, she jumped out from her spot and onto the walkway that would lead her to the back entrance enclosed by a tall curtain wall, her only outdoor safe haven. A hint of lavender mixed with a sooty smoke burned her nostrils as she inhaled. She tasted the scent, a pleasant floral mixed with the slightest of grit and ash from a nearby hearth.

From the outside, the abbey looked as though its spires could touch the sky, nearly a score of windows and more atop its stone walls casting out a glow of light and hope throughout the land. It was a beacon in the night alit with torches, a sanctuary for all who came for its wisdom. How she hoped it would protect her from the cruelty she'd found herself in, a cruelty she'd found shocking and painful. She stood and hugged herself, so grateful for those who had brought her to this spot, this safe haven of the Lord.

She had arrived at this heavenly retreat with bloodied knees, sore arms, cheeks reddened from the slap of a large hand. She wished to never leave, the cold stone as comforting as her mother's warm embrace so many years ago.

Breathing deeply of the outdoor air, she smiled at the freshness, the sweetness, of the lovely day, enraptured by the fading sunshine lighting the leaves on the ground. She'd always taken pleasure from the smaller things in life, finding beauty in the mundane and familiar.

Cadyn MacAdam had his back to her, his muscles rippling through the tight tunic he wore as he lifted a huge boulder up and over his head before dropping it to the ground. What was he doing?

"Cadyn?" she whispered after the boulder fell to the ground. "Am I interrupting you, my lord?"

He spun around quickly to face her, wiping the sweat from his fair brow with his plaid, and smiled at her in welcome. "Nay, no' at all. Without my companions to train with, I lift to keep myself strong. My clansmen give me a bit of chaff for the unusual way I exercise my body, but it helps me to build strength and endurance, something they appreciate in battle."

Staring at the boulder, she wondered if it would help her.

"Aye, it probably would be good for ye to build some muscles as well," he explained as if he read her mind. "But ye would probably start with something smaller," he added with a grin.

A rare smile broke out across her face. Since her father pulled her from her aunt and uncle's home in the Borderlands to deliver her to her betrothed's home in York, she'd had very little to smile about. "Perhaps I will attempt it soon. Do you have a moment to discuss something with me? I can arrange to return at another time if you wish to continue your task of lifting boulders." She brushed the imaginary wisp of hair from her face, knowing she did it only because it kept her fingers from touching the blond hairs that had fallen into Cadyn's eyes.

Ladies did not touch men. She sighed because she'd already failed at this twice. But the threat of the baron had made her act without thinking.

Besides, his heat had warmed her through, and the hardness of him made her realize that the baron should indeed fear this man.

She jumped, the loud sound of a fist pounding on the front door startling her even before she heard her father's voice demanding entrance. How had he made it through the gate? Cadyn pivoted to stand in front of her, a protective move that she appreciated.

Cadyn was fully aware of the situation she was in and had pledged to protect her, but could he, a Scotsman, take arms against the English? She tugged on her plait, wishing she could stop the terrible thoughts and fears that raced through her mind, her present state proved to be a turmoil that would not relent, leaving her confused and dazed too often. "Why would they come for me knowing this is an abbey? Now they have both attempted to remove me."

"Dinnae worry. I'll no' allow either of them to remove ye from the premises." He stood in front of her, his back guarding her, his legs wide, as he faced the front of the abbey. She leaned against him, perhaps a bit too intimate, but touching Cadyn calmed her. He was her rock in this world where nearly everything she knew to be true had turned upside-down. He looked down at her, his warm breath heating her. "He'll no' touch ye, I promise."

His words came out in a whisper that swept through her, caressing her as though she were the finest flower in the vase. She sighed, hoping he hadn't noticed.

A nun they knew as Eda moved to the door to peek out through the small opening. "Who is banging so harshly in the house of our Lord? And so late in the day? Go away and return after the sun is rising on the morrow, if you please." The passageway from the front of the abbey to the back was short, making it easy for the two of them to see who banged at the door. She feared stepping any closer lest she be grabbed and forced out the front entrance.

Despite being completely concealed, tucked as she was behind Cadyn's muscular presence, Tryana had the sudden sensation that her sire would see her, would know she was just beyond the back door. Silently, she moved closer to the stone wall at her back and shifted into a hiding place she'd chosen the first day they'd arrived. It was behind a bush against the abbey, a small nook she could squeeze into where she hoped to not be noticed.

"Ye need no' hide. I'll protect ye," Cadyn assured her quietly. He stood in front of the bush, his hands now on his hips. "Do ye no' trust me, lass?"

Why she allowed the fear to consume her so, she'd never know. "I know you will, my lord, but please forgive me. I feel safer back here. I cannot explain myself."

Cadyn nodded and said, "Since ye have a solid hiding place, I'll go speak to him." He was the only person inside the abbey allowed to carry a weapon, and his hand settled on the hilt of his large sword before he stepped back into the passageway of the abbey, his large frame filling the doorway.

Tryana did her best to arrest the tears that threatened to flow down her cheeks. She stared up at the gray sky, listening carefully, though she needn't be worried because her sire's voice carried back to her as clearly as if he'd been standing in front of her chastising her as he was wont to do.

"I want my daughter."

CHAPTER TWO

TRYANA DID HER best to keep from trembling, her father's voice seeping through her like the hiss of a snake.

The nun acted innocently enough by asking her father who he was searching for, but Cadyn put an end to the charade. "She will no' be leaving the abbey, de Gray. 'Tis her choice and I'm here to see that her will is followed." The sound of Cadyn unsheathing his sword was as clear as her sire's voice.

"You conniving bastard," her father said, the gasp from Sister Eda loud enough for her to hear.

"My lord, please remember in whose house you are standing. Do not curse in the house of our Lord." The nun was one of the timid ones, her thin frame nearly invisible under her robes. She prayed the woman would not faint.

Her father's voice carried loud and clear down the passageway, and Tryana recognized his usual tone of annoyance at dealing with a female. "Do not concern yourself with men's business, Sister. Stay out of this. Go back inside where you belong." She could hear the grating tone of her sire's voice, the same grate he used whenever he spoke of a woman's place.

She'd never seen him treat any woman kindly, especially her dear mother. Why would a nun be any different? She stepped out of the bush and peeked around the corner to see where her father stood. His face was as red as she'd ever seen it, the vein in his forehead popping out. Tryana tried to will her heart to stop beating so fiercely.

"Who the hell are you?" Wrath de Gray asked Cadyn.

"Cadyn MacAdam of Clan Ramsay. I volunteered to protect yer daughter, and I am a man of my word."

"Two silver coins to you to hand her over to me right this moment, no questions asked."

Cadyn snorted. "Ye dinnae know anyone who is honorable, do ye? I gave my pledge to protect her, and I will see it through. Keep yer coin and take yer leave."

"As you wish for now," Wrath spit out. "But I will return on the morrow at high sun with her betrothed and his force of soldiers. We will drag her away if we must, and you will not be stopping us."

The nun said, "The Reverend Mother allows sanctuary for anyone who wishes it. The Lord says you must respect this tenet."

He turned to yell at the nun, his voice rising more with each word. "The Lord says she's my daughter and I'll do with her as I wish, but you have the same lowly mind she has so I'm not surprised you don't recognize my superiority. I will return on the morrow, and I will not leave without her."The last phrase came out in a bellow, each word slowed for emphasis.

The door slammed, causing Tryana to start, but she let out the breath she'd been holding. She moved into the doorway, watching Cadyn as he strode back down the passageway toward her. For some reason, Cadyn was not intimidated by her sire. That fact made her like him even more. She called out, "My apologies, Sister Eda." The frazzled nun whirled about and headed back inside. "Cadyn, we should leave. Poor Sister Eda. He will frighten her and any other nun inside the abbey. Yet he does not seem to upset you and that pleases me."

Cadyn said, "Yer sire is a man who likes to hear his own voice. Fear no', I dinnae allow that kind of person to upset me. He spends his day trying to intimidate others. I suspect beatings and whippings were commonplace at his estate."

Her eyes misted and she nodded. "I should not have put you through this."

"He doesnae upset me. Dinnae let his empty threats upset ye either. I would guess they dinnae have many guards."

Cadyn came to her side quickly, and she gripped his biceps, her sire's words taking on new meaning to her. "Cadyn, he's returning with soldiers. You know what that means, do you not? It means we must be ahead of him. I will not remain here and allow myself to be removed. He will do it. But I refuse to allow him to take me from here and hand me back to that evil man,

Gareth Ward. I think we should leave right away. Perhaps at dawn. Or in the early hours of the day. And I will ask you to teach me how to defend myself with a dagger."

Cadyn gave her a crooked smile, nodding his head in agreement with her request. "I'd be happy to teach ye how to defend yerself. But are ye sure ye wish to leave? And where will we go?"

"To my aunt and uncle's place in the Borderlands. My father rarely argued with Uncle Lowrans. He is my mother's brother." She had the sudden urge to lean her head against Cadyn's chest, as if that thick wall of muscle would protect her.

"And yer mother?"

"Died when I was ten. She fell down the staircase and hit her head." She didn't add that she'd just learned from her brother that her father had pushed her dear mother to her death. Even she had a difficult time believing the man to be so innately evil.

Cadyn thought for a moment. "I dinnae know if ye will be safe at yer uncle's. If ye wish to leave, I will insist ye travel with me to Ramsay land. Wulf said he would send men to escort ye. If we leave, we should run into them. I know their path so I assure ye, if they are on their way, I will find them. 'Tis the safest way for ye. Though 'twill take most of the day to make it back to Ramsay land, so staying at yer uncle's for one night could be a part of our plan if we are delayed for any reason. Does he have many guards?"

She shook her head. "He lives in a small hut. Large enough for us to sleep there, but he has no guards. If we are ahead of my sire, we could sleep there. At least, I would like to visit with him and tell him all that has transpired. My aunt and uncle would not like to see me married to a man like the baron. And they should know how upset my sire is. He could take it out on them if he cannot get close to me. He carries grudges for a long time."

She watched as Cadyn thought for a moment, scratching his beard, walking toward the rear of the curtain wall. He looked to be a man who needed to pace when he thought. He was attractive, with hair so fair that it nearly glowed in the fading light of early evening. He had a strong jawline and eyes the color of the dewy grass of spring. He was committed to his work, something Tryana admired more than anything. Lifting boulders to gain strength was an admirable trait. And she didn't mind the extra bulge in his shoulders and his upper arms.

But what Tryana admired the most about Cadyn was his protective nature. She had never felt safer than she had in the past week since Reyna had placed her under his protection. He made her feel safe and secure, especially after the trauma she had endured at the hands of the cruel baron. She had never felt such kindness before knowing Cadyn, and it made her heart swell with gratitude.

As she walked towards him, Cadyn stopped his pacing to lean against the wall, his arms crossed over his chest. He was staring out into the distance, his eyes narrowed in thought. When he heard her footsteps, he turned his head and smiled warmly at her.

"Tryana, please dinnae worry overmuch," he said, pushing himself off the wall and walking towards her. "I'll keep ye safe. Ye have my word, but I must advise against stopping at yer uncle's place. 'Twill no' be a safe place for ye since we have no guards. If ye persist in leaving, I must insist we go straight to Ramsay land as quickly as we can travel. I can return to yer uncle if ye wish, after I have ye safely behind the protection of Clan Ramsay's many guards."

Tryana shook her head. "My sire does not take kindly to anyone who stands in his way. He will find a way to return me to the baron. I am certain of it, yet as sure as I am about that, I am sure that I shall not return to the baron willingly. If he forces me to return, I shall run away. I may as well run now. There is little point in waiting for him to come for me. Better that he does not know where I am. I say we leave."

Cadyn's expression darkened. "I won't allow him to hurt ye or take ye away."

She reached for his forearm, rubbing the light hair before she grasped his wrist tight. "Cadyn, I beg you. We cannot wait. Cannot give him the time to gather forces. I suggest we shall leave in the middle of the night, the only time I can trust my sire will not be on the road looking for me. Do you agree, Cadyn?"

"How do ye know that?"

"Because my sire never interrupts his sleep. He will lock his door to make sure he is undisturbed each night. I'm certain of that. The middle of the night is the safest time for us to travel if you can lead the way." She nodded with emphasis, hoping to convince him that she knew what was best with her father.

Cadyn crossed his arms and said, "I will escort ye to Ramsay land but not to yer uncle's house. Unless we run into a large group of Ramsay guards along the way, then I must insist we move past the Borderlands. The best time to leave will be shortly after midnight. We'll make the decision as to where we go based on who we see along the way. When on a journey, one must be flexible. If we meet up with the Ramsay guards, we will be safe to do whatever ye wish. 'Tis my hope that we will find them quickly."

"Many thanks to you, my lord." It wasn't exactly what she'd hoped for, but close enough.

"Cadyn." His green eyes sparkled when he said this.

She had the feeling that she could grow to like Cadyn very much. First she'd have to be free of her father and the evil man who considered himself her betrothed.

She locked gazes with him, a sense of warmth washing over her. He stepped closer to her, his hand reaching out to touch her cheek. "Dinnae worry, Tryana," he said softly. "I willnae allow him to hurt ye. I swear on my honor as a Ramsay guard."

Tryana's heart swelled with gratitude as she looked up at him. She knew that he meant it, that he would do anything to protect her. She leaned into his touch, feeling his warmth and strength seeping into her.

"I trust you, Cadyn," she said, her voice barely above a whisper.

Cadyn's eyes met hers, and for a moment, everything else faded away. He leaned in closer, his breath hot against her face, and pressed his lips to hers in a soft, gentle kiss.

Tryana felt her heart skip a beat as she kissed him back, feeling a rush of heat and desire course through her body. She knew that this was wrong, especially since they were in an abbey, so she pulled back. The heat in his gaze made her wish she would be sleeping next to the man all through the night.

But they would be leaving soon.

Everything about this man who held her tight gave her more hope than she'd ever had before.

Cadyn gave her a quick kiss on her forehead. "I will chat with the abbess and the stable master to be sure we are well-prepared for our journey. Make yerself ready then and we should both try to get a short rest before we leave. We willnae wait long into the night to take our leave if ye wish to be far ahead of him."

"I will ready my things."

Cadyn took his leave while she headed back to her chamber.

But as her foot reached the first step of the staircase, she hesitated, then moved back out into the cool air so she could gaze up at the spire of Ellonton Abbey.

A sudden reminder of her youth overcame her,

warming her heart as to the importance of the church. Many years ago, they had lived close to Lochluin Abbey in Perthshire. She had loved that abbey. It was much different than Ellonton Abbey because Lochluin was considered a double abbey, holding both nuns and monks. Here there were only nuns, though many guards came to protect them along with other workers. Ones who helped keep the small abbey always looking its best.

Perhaps it was time for her to return to Lochluin Abbey, to the secret she held tightly within, never having shared with anyone.

Her mother had taken her to Lochluin Abbey often, especially whenever her father and Wulf had gone hunting or to market. There she'd learned to listen to the monks practice their singing, playing the lute and the harp. The sisters allowed her to peruse the library kept just for the nuns. She'd grown to love the smell of the book bindings, the touch of the worn pages, and the words that took her away from her own life and into another.

Books had been her escape for many years—escape from her mother's tears and her father's cruel words. They'd become her favorite place in the world—the place she could launch a ship out to sea, stroll into a fairy garden, or have tea with special friends—all without leaving the chair in the library. Sometimes her mother would find her lying prone on the floor, her elbows holding her up so she could immerse herself in a world of animals or girls her own age or kings and queens of the royal court. Each journey was as transcendental as the next.

Then her mother would gather her up and take her back to her true world full of fear and chores and tears.

Perhaps it was time to return to Lochluin Abbey after she found her way back to Ramsay land.

She spun around to return to her bedchamber but something stopped her in her tracks, the sight of a shooting star darting across the night sky catching her eye. Her mother had told her that a shooting star was a message from the angels in the heavens. She recalled the first time her mother had told her this. She'd innocently asked, "But what is the message, Mama?"

"The message is the answer to whatever you need most at the time. It may be a message to take action on whatever thought you were having just then. Always remember what you had been considering just before it appeared. That will tell you the message."

She'd been thinking on two subjects. One was to return to Lochluin Abbey soon, and the other had just popped into her head.

She couldn't wait until the middle of the night. It was time to leave on her own. She'd eat supper as always, then take her leave. After all, she'd been alone all those years ago when she'd snuck away to Lochluin Abbey. It was not fair to risk everyone else's well-being over a few hours.

And she had to stop at her dear auntie's house and warn her of her sire. Cadyn wasn't going to allow that. It was time to go on her own.

Tryana stopped at the chapel before she returned to her room, making sure to say a prayer for a safe journey for the two of them. For she was certain that once Cadyn learned that she'd taken her leave, he would follow. It was very important to her that Cadyn remained safe since he'd volunteered to be her protector. And what a fine one he'd been. Making the sign of the cross, she made peace with her decision and said one last prayer for guidance along the way.

Then she made her way to her chamber, packing her meager belongings into a small sack she had placed behind her saddle. She would speak to the abbess at the evening meal rather than bother her now.

But she would leave on her own, a few hours ahead of their plan. She had to get to her uncle's house to warn them. And to get her mother's special Bible that she'd left there. It was the only book she had that was truly hers.

And the baron would not take this one away.

CHAPTER THREE

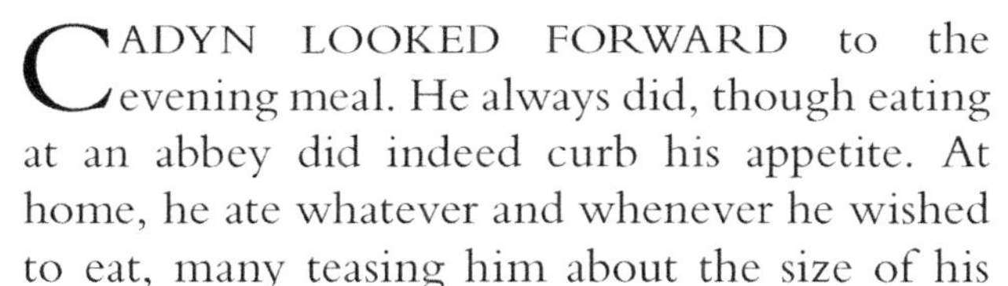

CADYN LOOKED FORWARD to the evening meal. He always did, though eating at an abbey did indeed curb his appetite. At home, he ate whatever and whenever he wished to eat, many teasing him about the size of his helpings. But eating pleased him.

He couldn't be that free in the abbey.

He entered the small hall they used for dining, pleased to see that Tryana had already seated herself. She'd freshened up and fixed her plait, a lovelier lass he'd not seen. He smiled and took the seat opposite her at the trestle table. One of the sisters who they hadn't been introduced to came in and placed a platter full of cheese and dark bread on the table for them, along with two small plates.

She said, "The abbess is resting and Sister Eda is not feeling well, so you will be alone this eve. I'll be in and out to take care of whatever you need, but I'll also be visiting with the others. Come to the kitchen if you need anything. Your beverage is on the chest."

After she left, Cadyn got out of his chair and

headed to the sideboard. "I think we have wine or mead. Would ye like a goblet of wine, Tryana?"

"Aye, if you please."

He set the goblet down for her and then his own before he sat. "Odd that we are alone in a place with so many nuns, but it pleases me."

"The nuns probably eat together. This hall is meant for guests." She took a small bite of the cheese. "Mmm. Abbey food is sometimes the best."

"Do ye think so? We had a chapel, no abbey to judge by. The priest was my uncle. He's getting mighty old in his years, but he is a fine man. Father Rab is a wonderful priest." He broke off two pieces of bread and offered her a piece that she took and set on a small plate in front of her.

"Tell me, Cadyn. What are your plans for your life? I wonder what kind of man you hope to become? What interests you have?"

Cadyn paused before he spoke, wondering how to explain exactly how driven he was by his hopes. Somehow, he felt like sharing with her, something he rarely did. "Everyone likes to accuse me of trying to imitate my grandsire because I walk like him. I do even follow him often. And the truth is I do wish to be like him, but I canno' help the way I walk, though no one believes me. But he was a spy for the Scottish Crown when he was young. I'd always dreamed of being the same."

"Truly? But that would take you away from Ramsay land, would it not?" She tipped her head and watched him, her blue eyes focused on him and only him. Something rare in his life simply because so much always happened in the Ramsay great hall.

"Aye, but I'd mostly like to train with him, but he is getting on in years. I dinnae know how much longer he'll be traveling. 'Tis harder for him now. He moves a bit slower, though his mind has no' slowed at all."

Her voice softened and she kept her gaze on her food. "Have you no plans to marry and have bairns? Or are you married already? Perhaps betrothed to a nice lass?"

Her question surprised him because it wasn't something he ever gave much thought to, though it was certainly a fair question. "I suppose someday, but I am neither betrothed nor married. What about ye? What are yer hopes and dreams?"

She let out a sigh, then smiled as if she were caught at something. "I have not thought much on it since this horrid betrothal, but it certainly has changed my thoughts. I just wish to live alone. I have one wish. That is to return to Lochluin Abbey, but I hope I can accomplish that soon. But only if we can rid ourselves of two nasty men."

"Why Lochluin?"

"We lived close to the abbey for many years, and it holds a special place in my heart. But there's something I must take care of. I have waited too long."

"Hopefully, yer sire will see his efforts are fruitless. Then I'd be happy to escort ye to Lochluin Abbey."

"I would like that."

They made small talk for the rest of their meal because the nun returned. When they finished, Cadyen said, "I shall knock on yer door when I am ready."

She nodded, unwilling to speak the lie.

She'd be long gone by then.

Unable to sleep, Tryana fussed about her chamber, making sure she had everything she would need. After hearing about Sister Eda at dinner, she knew she'd made the right decision. It was not right to put the sisters or the abbess at risk. Though she feared leaving the safety of the abbey and its solid stone walls, she knew that leaving was the right thing to do.

Warning her aunt and uncle was also the right thing to do. She would warn them, then head to Lochluin Abbey. If she knew how to get to Ramsay land, she might plan on stopping, but she had no idea where it was. If she were to guess, Cadyn would catch up to her right after she left her aunt and uncle's because that would bring her back to the main path.

And she had no idea where to go from here other than to head straight east to the main path through England, then north to the Borderlands. Once there, she would recognize landmarks and find her way to her uncle's house.

Then she reminded herself that Cadyn had said he was a strong tracker. He would find her before she was ready to leave probably.

She waited until all was quiet, then headed

down the staircase. Proud of herself for grabbing a piece of cheese to stick in her bag while Cadyn had grabbed their drinks, she was confident she wouldn't starve. Heading out into the cool night with her mantle wrapped tight around her, she was not surprised to see Cadyn had their horses at the ready for them.

That made her departure even easier because she wouldn't have to step inside the stable.

How she regretted not having the chance to thank everyone at the abbey, but she hoped they would understand. She'd told Sister Eda enough about the baron for her to understand why she was requesting to stay. She hadn't used Ward's name when referring to the devil, but she guessed the nun knew exactly her meaning. Both men were ruthless and while they both claimed to be in favor with God, their actions spoke differently.

Gareth Ward had taken the Bible from Tryana's hands with the comment, "You are too ignorant to read, so there is no reason for you to have a Bible. Even if you could read it, you would not understand the teachings of the Bible. You are not of the favored class, instead advised to submit and do whatever your father and your husband tell you to do. This is not subject to discussion." He'd taken her dear book and stomped on it, something she'd apologized to God for many times over.

As soon as she'd arrived at the abbey, Mother Eleanor had gifted her with an even finer Bible. She'd admitted to lying to her father, a sin for certain. "Mother Eleanor, I confess that I have never told my father that I am able to read. My mother taught me and advised me to keep it a secret from all men, especially my father."

Mother Eleanor had patted her hand still holding the book tight against her chest. "I think God would forgive this one. I can see clearly that it was for your own safety that your mother told you so. Godspeed with you, wherever this journey of yours takes you, my dear. You are welcome to stay as long as you need."

Grateful that she'd not received penance for her sin, she said, "Many thanks for your hospitality. We do appreciate your warm welcome."

"May God bless both of you."

She felt guilty for not saying farewell, but the abbess would understand. It was time for her to leave, marking a sort of transition, an important change in her life.

From now on, she would refuse to cower to anyone.

CHAPTER FOUR

CADYN AWAKENED FROM a sound sleep, something in the night alerting him. He moved over to the window, opened the shutter just in time to see a horse heading down the path.

And it was not a man riding that horse.

Hellfire, but she'd snuck out ahead of him. He'd had a suspicion, so he had planned to get up earlier than he'd told her, but he'd hoped he was wrong. Apparently, the lass was a wee bit stubborn. And if he were to wager, it would be that her reasoning had something to do with Cadyn's wish to skip stopping at her aunt and uncle's place.

No matter. He'd already packed his things and readied the horses in anticipation for such an event, though Cadyn prided himself for always being at the ready. He'd catch her in no time at all.

Cadyn caught up with her in less than an hour, and he was genuinely pleased and impressed when she chose to hide in the forest to allow him to pass. She probably had no idea who was behind her.

He stopped his horse and said, "Tryana, ye may come out now." He didn't have to wait long before she appeared in front of him, her shoulders slumped. With guilt or because she hadn't wished to be caught, he didn't know.

"Ye didnae believe me when I gave my word to yer brother that I would protect ye, did ye? Or is it that ye dinnae understand what honor means to me?" He wasn't truly angry with her, but more impressed that she had the gumption to leave on her own. "But I dinnae think ye would travel alone. That does surprise me."

"I have before."

"I was unaware of that, but I'm sure I know why ye chose to leave. And I will offer ye the same as before. If we are able to do so safely, we will stop at yer aunt and uncle's place."

"Please. My aunt has my mother's Bible, and I would like to keep it, even though the abbess gave me a new one. And I need to warn them. I know it was wrong to leave ahead of you, but I just could not deal with the sister being ill, and who really knew why the abbess was not about? I'm sorry, but I'm babbling. I do that when I don't know what to say. But we needed to leave. And honestly, I'm glad you caught up with me. There are many sounds in the middle of the night."

He just couldn't be upset with her after all she'd been through. "We can chat as we ride. Ye willnae fight me?"

"I trust you, Cadyn." She brought her horse abreast of his.

"Then we must keep moving." They left and

Cadyn took the lead. The night was dry and they had the light of half the moon, something that aided their travel. They managed to move along efficiently for three hours before stopping in the dark of night. "Shall we rest for a wee bit? Neither one of us slept much before our journey."

Cadyn helped her down from her horse, then found her a private spot to take care of her needs while he turned his back. When they were both finished, he brought out a skin of mead and offered it to her while they settled in order to enjoy a part of the loaf Cadyn had taken from the leftovers of their meal.

"Cadyn, you were thinking as I was. I have a good chunk of the cheese." She smiled at him, and it struck him how lovely she was, especially with a smile on her face, her white teeth nearly brilliant in the middle of the night. He found a tree stump and brushed it off before covering it with one of his extra plaids. "Please have a seat, my lady."

She cast him an odd glance, and he understood immediately. "Tryana," he corrected.

"My thanks. How long before we arrive at my uncle's in the Borderlands?"

"Ye described a place not far from Berwick so I believe we should be there before high sun. I had hoped to run into a group of Ramsay guards by this point, but I see no evidence of them."

"Do you not think it is for the best that we are not seen together?" She did her best to rearrange her skirts, but they'd become quite wrinkled on the ride.

He scowled then said, "I dinnae think this qualifies for the regular rules of company. These are special circumstances."

"I would agree with you completely, but I am certain my father would not. Even my uncle will have questions. Perhaps we should come up with an explanation," she said, taking a bit of the brown bread and chewing slowly.

"I am hopeful we will come upon the Ramsay group. This will take care of any wagging tongues as Aunt Brenna would say. I am prepared to take the consequences of my actions. If yer father finds us and insists that I marry ye because I have compromised ye, I will do it." He took a swig of mead and scanned the area for any movement.

Shocked at the extent of his honor, she'd not have him forced into marriage because she had insisted they leave the abbey. That was not fair to him at all. "Nay, you will not be expected to do any such thing. My father does not control me any longer. I will answer only to my brother or my aunt and uncle."

"Wulf understands our need for traveling quickly, but yer uncle may not. Ye must consider this."

"I will not hold you to such a foolish commitment."

"'Tis no' such a bad idea. Marrying me would rid ye of the obligation to marry the baron. If I admitted to compromising yer reputation, we could marry in less than a sennight."

He could tell by the look on her face that this thought truly surprised her. She stumbled with her words as she did her best to come up with a fair argument against their marriage.

He knew he wasn't on the list of the most desirable bachelors on Ramsay land, but he thought his looks were fine enough. Many said he had the good looks of his mother though he would have preferred to have his sire's rugged appearance. His mother had told him several times that since his beard had come in thicker, he resembled his father now. He also had the Ramsay green eyes so many were jealous of in his family.

But his hair was light and rarely stayed in place. Instead it looked mussed up most of the time, sometimes even turning wavy in the heat of summer. He often left his beard a bit scruffy because he did not have the time to trim it. He had no idea how a lady like Tryana would feel about that.

"I would not allow you to commit to such a thing. It would definitely be the wrong reason to start a marriage. Why, we barely know each other."

"Did ye know the baron well?"

She frowned, telling him he'd guessed right on that point. "Obviously not. So I would like to put some questions to you, if you do not mind. Tell me something, Cadyn. Is your father kind to you? Does he give you good advice? Does he spend much time explaining to you what his plans are for you? What is your father's name?"

Cadyn arched a brow at her flurry of questions, but decided he should answer her. "My sire is

Cailean MacAdam and he is a fair man. He and my mother, Sorcha Ramsay, often talk about their hopes for us, for me and my sister Ceit. And our youngest sister, though she is but five summers."

"And what are their hopes for you and your sisters?"

He shrugged, not having given it much thought before. "They mostly wish us happiness. Hope we'll marry and be happy. My grandsire is the more difficult one to please. He has quite a reputation as the beast of the Highlands when he was younger and spying for the Scottish Crown, but now he is calmer."

"Will they choose your sister's husband for her? Choose your wife?"

He couldn't stop his eyes from widening at the thought. "Nay. We choose our own spouses. 'Tis something Aunt Brenna insists on. Says her mother made her promise to let her bairns choose their own spouses. And Uncle Alex does the same. All my cousins chose their own spouses."

"I wish I could choose my own husband."

"Ye dinnae know the baron at all?"

"Nay. I believe Papa was given a generous coin payment for me. Basically, he sold me to the highest bidder. That is what my brother thought would happen because my father is such a gambler. Said he was saving me for when he owed someone too much coin."

"He never asked ye for yer thoughts about Gareth Ward?"

"Nay, but..."

"But what? I'll never share yer secrets."

She brushed her hair back away from her face, fussing with things that weren't there. Clearly, this topic unsettled her. He waited, giving her the time she needed to consider her answer.

Finally, she replied, "He has never asked my opinion about anything. Men are more intelligent than women is his belief."

Cadyn thought about that for a moment, the implications so far-reaching that it conjured up multiple images in his mind. Grandmama arguing with Grandpapa, Aunt Brenna with Uncle Quade, Maggie with Will, Bethia with Donnan. Why, he couldn't even fathom his father daring to say that to his mother. He actually grinned at the thought.

"That amuses you?"

Cadyn was horrified he'd been caught. "Nay, ye dinnae understand. Please allow me to explain. I was thinking about what my mother would say if Da told her she wasn't as wise as he was, or Grandmama hearing the same from Grandpapa. They would never allow such a comment to be said..." He chuckled, unable to stop himself. "My family does no' believe that at all. They would concede that men are better swordsmen because of their strength, but our best archers are mostly women. Many in my clan believe Aunt Brenna is the smartest of all. She's a healer and her daughter Jennet is also very wise."

"Truly? Because my sire has always considered me dimwitted. And the baron took my Bible from me, telling me I am too ignorant to read."

"That makes me angry. Aunt Brenna would tell

him a thing or two. She and her brothers and sister vowed to teach everyone they knew how to read if they chose to. Their mother had taught them so they passed it on."

"So you are able to read?"

"Aye. Of course. And my sister and my cousins. Aunt Molly taught many of us. She was the best teacher of all."

Tryana's head fell forward as she stared at her hands in her lap. "I wish I were part of your clan, Cadyn."

"Never ye mind. I'll help ye get to yer aunt's place, whether now or after yer sire stops bothering ye, and she will allow ye to read all ye like. Aye?"

"Aye. We do not have many books, but I have a new Bible from Mother Eleanor." She swiped at the tears on her cheeks. "We must hurry before my sire is along. I do not wish to see how he treats you. You are a fine man, Cadyn MacAdam."

"My thanks. I'll do everything I can to get ye home safely," he said. "We will probably soon be joined by Chief Torrian and his guards so there will be no question. I hope so, or I fear it could be too risky to stop at yer uncle's home. I know this is yer preference, but we may have to go to Ramsay land, gain some guards, then back to yer uncle's house. Will ye accept that if I deem it too risky, lass?"

"I will. I prefer to be safe."

They mounted up and continued north toward the Borderlands. For the rest of their short time, they made small talk, focusing on family names and directions. They didn't spend much time in any one place because Cadyn feared they might be followed. They traveled for about one hour after the sun came up when the sound of hoofbeats could be heard coming toward them.

Tryana froze and stared at him. "Who could it be?"

Cadyn took the reins of her horse and led the animal into a clearing behind a copse of trees. "We shall see who it is."

It didn't take long before the group came abreast of them. His father bellowed out, "Cadyn! I know ye arenae far. Show yerself."

Tryana looked at Cadyn with a grin of relief. "You know him?"

"'Tis my sire. Come, I'll introduce ye."

They came out of the bushes to greet the two score guards that his chieftain had gathered, but his sire was in the lead. "Cadyn? What the hell are ye doing with a lass alone?"

Torrian, his chieftain, pulled abreast of his father, both directly in front of Cadyn. "Greetings, my lady. Fare thee well? Ye arenae hurt?"

"I am fine."

His father's temper did as it often did: jumped to conclusions. "Are ye out of yer mind escorting a lass alone? Ye know what the whole world thinks. Are ye prepared to marry the lass?"

"Aye, if she wishes, I would, but Papa, calm down. Her sire threatened to return her to the baron, her betrothed, who Reyna had rescued her from last week. Her father came to the abbey today, threatening the nuns and promising to return with a slew of the baron's guards. We snuck away last night and have been searching for ye along our journey. We were planning to go to Ramsay land if we dinnae find ye on the path, then she wishes to visit her aunt and uncle. Indeed, I expected ye sooner. What took ye so long?"

"Confusion," Torrian said. Turning to Tryana, he went on, "Wulf and Reyna wish to go after yer father, but they have delayed the trip due to Wulf's injury, though they cannae return to England. We'll escort you to Ramsay land now then."

"Wulf's injury? I saw him and he was hale. I asked him if he was hurt," Tryana said, her face now contorted with worry.

Torrian replied, "He took a leg wound and it became pus-filled. He'll be fine, but he is limping for now. My stepmother fixed him with her poultices. Dinnae worry about him. He is in the best place to heal, but only if he remains for a few more days."

"I pray he is hale," Tryana said. "If it's possible, I would like to visit my aunt and uncle first, see if they are hale. I know not exactly what games my father is playing. I pray he has not hurt them, but I would like to see for myself. Then I would visit Wulf and Reyna on your land if you can protect me from my father and the baron."

Torrian glanced over at Cailean. "We can do as ye wish for now. We shall escort ye to yer aunt and uncle's place, my lady. But only for a short visit."

"Please call me Tryana."

"Cadyn will also call ye the lady that ye are." Then his father cast him a harsh glance.

Cadyn ignored his father and rode at the outer side of Tryana, wishing to make sure no one would come out of the brush to surprise her. "Her aunt and uncle live just outside of Berwick."

"On Scottish land?"

"Aye. I was hopeful Wulf would be there now. I am worried for him."

"Nay, he is still healing. He's on Ramsay land with strict instructions from Brenna not to leave yet," Torrian explained. "And ye know no one ignores Brenna's instructions. Even if he thinks on it, Reyna will stop him. Plus her parents are said to be on their way here. Maitland told them not to return to Berwick for at least a sennight, I believe."

"I am grateful that you are willing to take me to visit my aunt. She is holding my mother's Bible, and I would like to retrieve it. Also, I believe it is important to warn them that my father is on the rampage, that he is furious because I have refused the betrothal. They need to know everything in order to stay safe. Perhaps they could visit her sister who lives near Inverness. My father would never bother them there."

Torrian assured her, "We will make a brief stop, and I will repeat that I do mean brief. Then we will go on to Ramsay land, and ye can see Wulf and Reyna with yer own eyes."

"This pleases me. It is all I am asking for now,"

Tryana said, her eyes misting and her hands clasping together.

Cadyn didn't say anything, but he knew in his gut that it was all up to him now.

He had to protect Tryana. He just hoped his sire didn't get in the way.

CHAPTER FIVE

TRYANA WAS VERY uneasy as they approached her uncle's hut. It was a big enough hut for the two of them, but there were no extra guards or any special protection. He lived in a small village and they protected each other, if necessary, though it had never been necessary in Tryana's mind. The others were a short distance away, and very few were outside working. Something unusual for this time of day. Had her sire already appeared to bother these poor people?

They started down the path but Tryana halted her horse as soon as she caught a glimpse of something behind the hut.

Someone was there.

Cadyn said to her, "I will check to see who it is. Yer uncle's name?"

"Uncle Lowrans and Aunt Canny." Her hand came up to her mouth as she watched the group of Ramsay guards do what they do best.

One word from Chief Torrian sent them off in different directions. Soon they had surrounded the hut while Cadyn went around back, but he returned quickly.

"No one is there, just horses. They must be inside." Cadyn dismounted and strode over to Tryana's horse. "Would ye like to greet yer aunt and uncle or shall I check first? If yer sire were here, would ye leave?"

She let out a big sigh. Cadyn asked an important question and she would answer it honestly. If her sire were truly here, she would speak to him and try to explain to him why she did not wish to be married to the baron. He knew nothing of her bloodied knees or her penance of carrying heavy books up and down the staircase until she passed out from exhaustion. There was no point in mentioning the removal of her Bible because her sire didn't know she could read.

Her mother had made her promise never to tell her father.

"Nay, I would speak to him. I will go inside."

She moved to the door, Cadyn behind her, his chieftain behind him. Torrian said, "Ye will no' be mistreated by yer father or yer betrothed, no' while we are here."

She smiled at the man and nodded, whispering, "My thanks to you."

She knocked on the door because she had no idea who would be inside. Her belly churned over the multiple situations she could encounter.

Her father answered the door. "I've been waiting for you. Get inside." Her father was always too quick to speak. He paused as though he just noticed the group of Highlander guards behind her.

Cadyn said, "She'll no' be coming inside until ye promise to treat her kindly."

"Of course, I will," he said, his gaze shifting from Cadyn to the tall man behind her and the monstrous horses behind him, a few now prancing as if impatient to get on with their work. "Tryana, I am pleased you are here. Your aunt is very worried about you. Please come inside."

Aunt Canny came to the door, her eyes widening as soon as she saw the group behind her. Then a small smile crept across her face. "Please come in, Tryana, and both men behind ye." The others were still on their horses.

Cadyn said, "I'd be glad to join ye." He allowed Tryana to step inside first, then set her carefully aside before checking the rest of the hut. Sure enough, he pushed a man out of the bedchamber, whom he guessed to be her betrothed.

"Ye have someone hiding inside, Aunt Canny," he said, Tryana covering her mouth with her hand to hide her smile at the baron's attempt to being sneaky was uncovered by Cadyn from the start. The fact that he hid in a bedchamber told her much about his character.

And if she were to guess, the man held a fear of these brawny Highlanders who had escorted her here.

The baron stood tall and said, "I was taking a brief rest. Why, there you are, my sweet. I have missed you terribly."

The baron came over to stand next to her, but

Cadyn stood fast by her side while the chieftain stood on her other side, neither allowing him to get close enough to touch her.

"Tryana," her father said. "Tell these fools he is your betrothed, Gareth Ward."

Torrian unsheathed his sword at the same time Cadyn unsheathed his. The echo of another score of swords unsheathing on the other side of the door carried to them, Wrath de Gray paling at the reminder there were many others outside the door.

"This man is a proud member of my clan, and he is no' a fool. Ye will speak with respect, or I shall teach ye what respect means." Torrian's gaze would have sent her back three steps at the least, but her sire didn't move, just sending a furious gaze his way, though it did not work on the large Highland chieftain.

"Send them away," Wrath said, not to anyone specific, but to both Torrian and Cadyn. Cailean came in the door and stood behind Cadyn. She couldn't help but notice her father's gaze dart to the outside, the line of Highlanders surrounding the house clear to anyone.

"I thought I would join my son and my chieftain," the man said with a smirk just before he set a dagger between his teeth.

Tryana had to fight not to giggle. Cailean was a touch taller than his son, though Cadyn had the more muscular physique with arms like tree trunks.

"We'll not be leaving until the lady makes the request. And ye will be treating her with respect, or I'll be teaching ye what that means." Chief Torrian stood tall without hesitation, his emotions unreadable through his powerful gaze.

"I think we may need to teach the baron how to treat a lass respectfully, Chief." Cadyn squared his shoulders and kept himself close to Tryana, something that calmed her. But the fact that he was about to stand up to these two cruel men for her meant even more. "The lady tells me she has bloodied knees from his demand that she pray in penance, kneeling on the stones for hours. I also noticed a bruise on her cheek as if someone had dared to slap her. 'Tis true, Baron? Have ye struck the lass intentionally? Because if ye have, I'll be happy to go outside with ye and show ye how I treat men who beat women. I promise not to use my sword but my fists only."

The baron paled, but said nothing, not wishing to take part in Cadyn's bold challenge.

Her father didn't pale but instead reddened so quickly that his fury was palpable. The man could build into a fury faster than a bolt of lightning shooting through a night sky. He used his words to try to incite fear instead. "You have no power over me. You Highland savages need to learn your place, and it's not to give anyone who is English nobility orders."

Torrian drawled, "Last I noticed we were still in Scotland, so we do have power. We are favored by our king, and ye arenae. So again I'll say treat her kindly, or ye can go outside and argue with my two score men on their warhorses."

"'Tis a favorite game of mine," Cadyn added.

"See who is faster, man or warhorse. Then see who is more powerful, man or beast. Care to meet the challenge, de Gray?"

Her father's face turned so red that she thought he was about to have one of those fits where people crumple to the ground and grab their heart, but he held firm. "Fine. We will be kind. Tryana, the baron would like to speak with you privately."

"I politely decline. I am no longer willing to marry the baron. Uncle Lowrans and Aunt Canny, the man forced me to pray on my knees on cold stone for many hours until my knees bled. Then he forced me to carry heavy books up and down the stairs until I dropped from exhaustion. I do not wish to live my life under such a cruel man."

"Cruel? I was testing you, my love. And you will suit me very well. You passed all of my tests. I just wished to see if you were made of a solid constitution, something that is important if you are to bear sons for me. I promise never to force you to kneel or carry books again. Please come back to my home so we can plan our wedding in a fortnight. All of my help are excited to have a new mistress in our home. Once you are with child, I'll no longer allow you to do any work at all. I'm hoping for three sons first, and then I'll allow you to have two daughters to help you care for the house."

"And the sons?" Cailean asked. "What will they do?" Tryana didn't know the man well, but based on the twitch in his jaw, she wouldn't have pushed the man. He apparently respected his daughter more than the baron would respect his own wife.

"Well, tend my books, of course. I'll teach them how to read and do numbers so they can manage all of my properties. Then someday they will take over my estate. If you honor me with three boys, I will forever be in your debt, my lady. The two daughters will help you care for all four of us."

Tryana teared up, unable to speak to this man whose beady eyes bore into her as a warning. If he spoke truly, he'd be telling her to do everything he said, or she'd be doing more penance. Every word he spoke felt like a threat though it was all veiled as kindness.

But did Cadyn and his chieftain believe him?

The baron tried to reach for her. "Please sit down. You must be exhausted from traveling." He tried to move to her side again, but Cadyn didn't budge.

"Just because she is a lass does no' mean she is weak," Cadyn said with a clenched jaw.

Tryana didn't wish to move from Cadyn's side, but Aunt Canny tugged on her arm and ushered her to the table. At least her legs would stop shaking if she were seated.

Her father said, "The Baron of Topcliffe and I both have a writ from the magistrate. Her betrothal to the baron has been announced, and the bride price paid so she must go with him and agree to the marriage or she will suffer due punishment that is decided by me. I have already spoken with my friend who is also a sheriff. He has agreed to imprison you for half a fortnight to consider your choices if you continue to refuse.

I do not think you would do well in a prison, my dearest daughter. It is in your best interest to go with us and marry. Your betrothal has been moved up to a sennight. No later."

Torrian asked, "May I see the writ from the magistrate, please?"

Her father handed the scroll over and Torrian looked at it, holding it out for Cailean and Cadyn. "Do ye wish to read it?" he asked Tryana when they finished.

When she reached for the parchment, her father swatted her hand down. "You are wasting your time. She cannot read. Turn her over, or I will have the sheriff take her into custody. He is on his way here now as a special favor to me. You know it will take time to prove any supposed law you are claiming to free her. It's a foolish claim because the contract between the baron and me has been signed. The female has no say in the contract, as you know. Not in England."

"True," Torrian said.

Tryana's hands began to shake. "But I'd like to become a nun. Please take me back to the abbey or to Lochluin Abbey so I can take my vows. I do not wish to marry." She looked from her aunt and uncle to her father and then to the baron and Cadyn.

But she knew the outcome.

Torrian said, "I'd like to speak to the lady privately along with Cadyn outside, if ye please. Cailean, ye will stay here until we return."

"Nay!" her father barked.

Torrian held his hand out to Tryana. "In this case, 'tis up to the lady. Tryana, what say ye?"

"Aye, I would like to speak with you alone." She stood and nearly ran out of the hut.

"If you take her, the sheriff will come for her. Ten lashes to her tender skin for running from a sheriff and disobeying her sire." Her father's voice carried strong out the door, and she shivered at the thought. She knew exactly how lashes felt.

She had no idea if her father was telling the truth or not, but she at least wished to speak privately with Cadyn.

Outside, Torrian led them away from prying ears. "Cadyn, I am sorry, but I dinnae think we can fight this writ. If Wulf were here, he might be able to argue this as her brother, but in England, 'tis the males in the family who have final say."

"Are we close enough that you could get my brother?"

"Wulf is still on Ramsay land and that is hours away due north. If he could be here, he would have come with us. His leg became infected so he is unable to ride a horse. We are in a bind. He cannot come to England because he is still wanted for murder. If ye are forced by the baron to go to York, we will need to find a way to get ye back on Scottish soil to stay. The baron sounds as if he realizes his mistake, and I think at this time he will not force ye to do anything like he did before. We will have to go to our king and gain permission to bring ye back to Scotland permanently. Unfortunately, he is in Ireland at present. This will take time, but I think we can do what we must within a sennight to gain yer freedom, lass."

"There must be another way," Cadyn said. "I gave my word to protect her. If I allow her to leave with the baron, then I have no honor. I understand the difficulty because Wulf is no' here and unable to come, but someone else should be able to speak on his behalf."

"Aye," Torrian explained. "The court would say her father is next in line. I understand yer concern, Cadyn, but I think our hands are tied until I get something from King Robert or we get Wulf to vouch for her. This can be accomplished in a short time, but not at the moment."

His father came outside to join them and said, "I fear no' with that writ. And a week in prison would be harder on ye, lass, than a week with the baron. 'Tis no' something they could get away with in Scotland, but many sheriffs are able to be convinced to do something short-term for a wee bit of coin. I suspect that is what is happening here. I agree with Torrian that after having been caught on his past behavior the baron will refrain from repeating his ill commands."

"But he cannot change," she pleaded. "There must be another way."

Cadyn crossed his arms and said, "She canno' go with them. His past cruelty proves it."

Torrian cast a stern eye at Cadyn, but then spoke to Tryana, "I didnae say he would change. If he marries ye, his twisted commands will continue until ye are with child, but I think he will refrain until ye are married. The law states ye must do whatever yer husband commands. Once ye say I do, ye are his to do with as he wishes."

Her eyes misted. "I do not wish to go with him."

Torrian said, "Cadyn, think of all we have learned about sheriffs. Consider what just happened to Grif."

"I do understand part of my chief's reasoning. If ye must go, ye would be safer with the baron. We've known of multiple instances of disreputable sheriffs, so I would hate to see ye with one. If yer father pays enough coin, he could get ye imprisoned. I dinnae like any of this, but we would have more difficulty gaining yer freedom from a prison than from the baron's small estate. We did it before, we could do it again," Cadyn said, taking her hands in his.

She'd heard awful tales of prisons in England. And what if she could never get out? Perhaps her better chance was with the baron. Her father would give her penance, but she did not think the baron would. Not until she was formally his wife.

"But I still believe ye should stay in our care. We shall take her back to Ramsay land where Wulf can help her. Da, do ye no' think this would be best?" Cadyn asked. "Chief? Will ye no' reconsider? I gave my word."

Torrian crossed his arms, his lips pursed. It was an expression that told her he did not like to be questioned. She did not want Cadyn to get in trouble because of something she had done. He'd protected her, gotten her to her uncle's home just as she'd asked. And he'd pressed her not to stop here. There was a small part of her that realized she was wrong in insisting to stop here.

That she had this coming. First the nuns, now Cadyn were taking risks for her. It was wrong. She thought for a moment, then did the only thing she could do.

She placed her hand on Cadyn's forearm. "I'll go with the baron. I will cause no more trouble. Please keep my father here."

"Then I will go with ye," Cadyn declared.

"Nay, Cadyn. Go find my brother. He will get me out of this mess. I wish this all to end." Tears misted her gaze, but she held them back. "Go to Ramsay land. For me." Before he could argue, she stepped inside the cottage.

"And ye have my word that we will come for ye before the sennight is up, lass," Cadyn said.

"I beg ye to come for me, Cadyn. Please." Her eyes misted, but she stared up at the gray clouds above to gain control. She would not allow her father to see her tears.

With that, she strode back into the hut and made her announcement.

She felt like she was going to her own funeral.

"I'm going with her." Cadyn moved over to his horse and mounted up.

His sire said, "They'll no' allow ye along. They have guards hiding behind the next cabin. Look beyond." His sire was correct. Four or five men a short distance away kept their gaze on all that was transpiring with Tryana. And there were horses behind the cottage that spoke of extra men somewhere.

"Then I'll follow on my own. I'm not leaving her to that bastard. Who knows what he will do? I must follow and see that she goes to York. What if they take her elsewhere? We'd never find her. I promised Wulf and Reyna."

His father said, "Absolutely no'. I forbid it."

Torrian said, "Let him go. He has a point. I would at least feel better if we could tell Wulf we knew exactly where she was. Cadyn can follow her back to York, though he'll have to hide because they'll never allow it, confirm that she is in residence at the baron's home, then return to us and we'll have Wulf at the ready. Once we get word that she is in York, we will deliver Wulf there and remove her from the baron's presence. No more than three days and she'll be back."

Cadyn didn't like leaving Tryana there, but his father and his chieftain convinced him he had no choice. Whether the writ was true or not was the first thing he needed to determine.

"Do ye think the writ was true, Chief?" he asked as soon as they were a short distance away from the cottage.

Torrian said, "Probably no', but the issue is that if they chose to go to their king, would Edward grant them the writ? Aye, I believe he would. Edward will do anything to upset the Scots so forcing a marriage to an English nobleman to keep himself in the favor of a baron? I believe he would provide it for them. And we have little weight to our argument. If she were a member of our clan, I might be able to argue more, but I have no evidence or claim to the lass."

"But the baron was cruel to her."

"If her sire didnae care, Edward willnae either. England gives no voice to the female. She is a bargaining coin only. Sad but true. And once she is married to him, she wouldnae be the first woman to be treated cruelly by her husband."

Cailean said, "Cadyn, we need to get her brother fit for travel. Wulf would have had a chance of fighting for his sister's rights. He could, at the verra least, attest to her treatment by the father and the baron. Without him, there is little we can do."

"Can we not get him to sign a writ of our own? That he does not approve of the marriage?"

Torrian said, "Dinnae forget he is wanted for murder. The English would declare he needed to show on their land and he would be arrested. We are in a bind, but we'll find a way out."

"Of course, we are assuming he is still back on Ramsay land. Dinnae forget that Maitland sent Dyna back to Ramsay land to let Reyna and Wulf know the two of ye were missing. We passed her along the way. By now, she has arrived and Wulf knows Tryana is gone. Who knows if he will wait once he learns she's missing."

"So Cadyn will follow the baron at a distance. Where do we suggest we go now?" Cailean asked. "Do ye have a plan, Chief?"

"Back to Ramsay land. I hope to catch Wulf before he leaves. We have to catch up with him."

"I will return as soon as I am certain of Tryana's safety in York," Cadyn stated.

"We will await yer update, Cadyn. Wulf will find a way to free his sister, I'm sure. And he has plenty who will help him. I didnae like the baron. We have a sennight to come up with a plan. Wulf will be healed by then."

"If no', I'll go after her myself." Cadyn gave his sire a look to let him know that he was serious. "Ye'll no' convince me otherwise."

CHAPTER SIX

TRYANA FOUND HERSELF back in the baron's care at his home within two days. After she'd stepped back inside her uncle's cottage without the Highlanders, her father had grabbed her arm and pulled her aside swiftly.

"I will warn you to do as you are bid, or you will pay the price. Take any other view but to do as your husband tells you, and I'll have you imprisoned." Those were her father's parting words. It suited her just fine because she'd prefer never to speak with him again.

She hadn't spoken to anyone once they left Berwick, even though she had the oddest feeling that they were being followed. Somehow, she didn't expect her sire would keep it a secret if he followed.

So who could have followed them? The Highlanders had definitely not followed because she'd glanced over her shoulder a few times and saw they did not move. They kept her sire back though, as promised, and her betrothed had rushed his guards along quickly, probably because unlike her sire, he'd demonstrated a true fear of the Highlanders. They'd moved along, only making one stop before they arrived back on his land.

She hoped to never see her father again. Thinking on all that had transpired, she now understood her father. He'd never loved either of them because he knew neither one were of his blood. Their mother had taken a lover.

Tryana had much time to think on the journey. She'd taken herself back to Lochluin Abbey, to all the times she'd gone with her mother for a visit. Her mother had often said she was going to say her prayers in the chapel and suggested Tryana wait for her in the library.

Her mother had known how easily entranced her daughter was with the many books in the library. And once the nuns had caught on to her joy, they'd found more and more books to suit her.

Now that she was more mature, she had to wonder what her mother had been doing all those times Tryana spent reading in the library. Praying for a short time, she didn't doubt, but it had been hours, if she were to guess.

She'd often seen one of the workers smile kindly at the two of them. He was a handsome man with the bluest eyes.

She nearly gasped at the thought. Blue like her own. Dark-haired like Wulf. Had her mother been in love with one of the workers at the abbey?

She had seen her mother with that man at the abbey, so it was certainly possible that he could be their father, but he'd never made any attempt to try to get to know either of them, so she decided whoever their true father was, he didn't deserve her love. Any true father would search out his children, make sure they were hale.

He had done nothing and deserved no effort from her or Wulf.

As they entered the baron's home, Tryana felt a sense of dread wash over her. She knew what awaited her here, and it wasn't pretty. The baron had made it clear that he would stop at nothing to make her into his submissive wife, and Tryana knew that she had to be careful if she wanted to survive.

The baron led her to a small chamber on the second floor. The room was sparsely furnished, with only a small bed, two stools, and a wooden chest for her belongings. The windows were shuttered, and the door was solid oak with a heavy lock.

As the baron closed the door behind him, Tryana knew that she was in trouble. She could sense the lust in his eyes, and she knew that he wouldn't let her go so easily. She tried to stay calm, to keep her wits about her, but it was hard when she was alone with him. As soon as he left, she crept over to the window, pulled the shutter back, and stared out over the landscape, wishing she were looking out over the fine hills of Scotland.

For a quick second, she swore she saw a man who looked like Cadyn MacAdam. She blinked and moved closer to peer out, but she couldn't be certain.

Just the thought of Cadyn spread a warmth to

her insides that she hoped to hold for a long time. And how she prayed he would rescue her from this frightful situation she found herself in again.

The door opened behind her and Tryana whirled around, then released a breath of relief as a maid entered the room. The baron stuck his head in long enough to speak to Tryana, "I will allow you to rest. You will stay here until I call for you. I'm sure you are exhausted. We'll talk on the morrow." Once he left, she glanced back out the window, but no one was there. She closed the shutter and took a seat on the bed.

The baron was an unremarkable man with nondescript features and a short stature. He had a receding hairline of dull brown hair that he kept well-groomed, and his face looked freshly shaven each time she saw him. His eyes were his least attractive feature, closeset and narrow with a muddy brown color that resembled rot, looking beady like the rats she'd seen in the dark tunnel. Both her sire and the baron valued their appearance and were lean of body, but only Cadyn put in the effort to keep himself fit by carrying boulders, something she couldn't picture the baron doing in her wildest dreams.

But here she was, back again in the home of the baron. If she married him, she had no doubt that she would become a prisoner in her own home, never leaving this building unless to attend kirk. How she prayed Cadyn would find a way to free her from this ugly situation.

The maid who entered was named Bess and informed her that she had taken over her care.

"We moved your belongings into this room in your absence, my lady."

Once inside her chamber, she said, "Where is the baron's bedchamber?" She imagined that she wouldn't be fortunate enough to have a hidden passage in this chamber as there had been in her previous room, and she wanted to know if she could make her way back to the secret passageway.

Her escape route would no longer be available to her.

"The baron's chamber is down the passageway. You will have the connecting bedchamber after you are married." Bess glanced over her shoulder as though to make sure no one was listening. In a lowered voice, she asked, "Where did you go?"

Tryana had no concern and actually thought the lass could be a friend. She appeared to only be a few years older than her nearly twenty years. She'd never had a friend at her home with her sire, and she kept to herself at her aunt and uncle's house. A friend would be welcome. "My brother stole me away. He heard about my bloodied knees and took me to a healer."

She had been treated by a healer at the abbey, so it was just a bit of a twist on the truth. Glancing down at her still scabbed knees, she was hopeful that the baron would not start her penance again in the morning.

"I had no idea the baron would treat you so poorly. He needs to have an heir or two, so he should treat you ever kindly until you give him those heirs. Then he would thank you every day. Men are foolish sometimes." Bess made an odd sound with her tongue indicating her dissatisfaction with her employer. "I'll have a bath set up for you, my lady, then you may rest."

Tryana nodded, not really caring what happened back in this awful home. She missed Cadyn desperately—the way he always watched over her made her heart squeeze. Since her mother died, no one had made her feel as safe and protected as Cadyn could. Her brother had tried to step in, but Wulf was driven by his own demons. She thought back on how protective Cadyn had been at her aunt and uncle's home, standing next to her when the baron tried to take her hand and pull her over next to him.

Cadyn would not allow it. No matter what her sire or the baron said, he stayed steadfastly by her side, as strong as the tallest tree in the forest. And he was so powerful looking that neither man dared to try to push him aside.

Her father pushed everyone around, and she guessed the baron probably did the same. Was it fear of Cadyn or the Ramsay chieftain that kept the two men from doing what they wished to do?

If up to them, she'd have been dragged out the door and tied to a horse, her hands bound. But the Highlanders spoke of something she was unfamiliar with.

Respect for a lass.

As far as she knew, her entire life was to be spent doing whatever some man bid her to do. Her mother did whatever her father had told her to do.

Nay, yelled at her to do. They'd had little friendly discourse.

Bess helped her into the bath, the steaming water relaxing her. "My lady, the baron has already left so you need not worry about him bothering you this eve. He often visits his brother at a tavern in the village."

"Bess, may I ask you something?" She looked up at the woman with kind eyes, those eyes the one feature that gave her hope that she could trust her, even though she was a maid and employed by the baron. She was neat and pretty, her rounded hips reminding Tryana of her mother.

"Of course. I'll answer if I can."

Bess washed her hair, her soothing ministrations calming her instantly. "Is the baron always cruel?"

Bess sighed and said, "I would call his ways harsh. And he does discipline any help who does wrong. Breaking dishes, not brushing the horses down, ruining dinner, those kinds of things. I was surprised he treated you so poorly. The help is never surprised by their treatment, but to treat a lady so poorly is inexcusable, especially since you are not married yet. We all felt sorry for you."

"He said he was testing me."

Bess nodded, considering her words before she spoke. "For your sake, I hope he was being honest. He needs to treat you better. Those books were impossible for a lass of your slight build to carry up and down the staircase. It was a task that served no purpose. Why, you could have fallen down the entire flight and snapped your neck. It was a most dangerous proposal."

Somehow, she doubted the man would change. In her opinion, he left to keep himself from treating her poorly for running away. It would be a challenge for him to keep away from her until they were married.

"Are you married, Bess?"

"Aye. And we have two beautiful daughters."

"Did you choose your husband?"

Bess let out an unladylike snort. "Of course not. But I've learned to care for Hal. He treats me kindly and I do the same with him. He's a good father and that is the most important characteristic to me."

Somehow, she didn't think the baron would have that characteristic.

She expected his cruelty to start up the day after they were wed. But it didn't matter. She had to return to Scotland. There was someone waiting for her there. She'd told no one about him. Not her brother, not Cadyn, not her father.

But she would find her way back, no matter what. Until that day, she had to behave so she wasn't totally destroyed. Cadyn and his chieftain said they would get her away before she was forced into marriage.

She had to be patient, and that could prove to be her greatest challenge.

Cadyn had followed the baron all the way back to his home in York, pleased to see that Tryana was where he'd said she would be. He'd noticed her at the window on the second floor, wishing he could call out to her, but he would not bring any more trouble down on the lass. He'd even waited long enough to notice that the baron had gone to a nearby tavern alone.

Once the bastard had taken his leave, Cadyn decided to return to Ramsay land. He would have preferred to speak with Tryana, but he needed to get back to Wulf in a timely manner. The more he thought about it, the more he believed that once Wulf received Dyna's news that they'd left the abbey, he might have gone out on his own.

He needed to speak with Wulf. So he headed back to Ramsay land, arriving back well after the sun was up the next day. He'd only stopped for a short rest because he was too intent on his mission. This was his one chance to show his sire and grandsire how trustworthy and honorable he was because he was acting alone.

He had to make them proud. See how strong a guard he was.

That discussion would come later. Once he arrived, he asked the stable lad, "When did the chief return?"

"Last eve before the evening meal. Chief went straight to his bed, told Cailean to tell Wulf he'd speak with them in the morn. He wished for ye to return before approaching Wulf. And Wulf was still with the fever so Reyna sent him to bed early. He didnae argue, so I was told by others."

He was pleased to hear Reyna and Wulf remained on Ramsay land, though he worried about his fever.

He stepped inside the hall, grabbed some food from the sideboard and a mead, then took a seat at the trestle table, the hall mostly empty. He wasn't there long before Reyna came down the stairs and stopped her descent once she saw him. "I'll get Wulf. Torrian said we had to wait for ye."

Wulf limped down the stairs a few moments later. He stood in the middle of the hall, his leg clearly still paining him, trying to decide where to sit.

"Wulf, sit at the table and prop yer leg up. I'll go find Torrian." Reyna hustled and bustled about just like her mother often did.

Wulf came along, pausing to ask him, "Ye know where she is?"

"Aye, she is with the baron in York."

Reyna joined him and Wulf grabbed onto her hand, clutching her tight as if Reyna were the only one who kept him from going daft. Torrian and Cadyn's father came into the keep from outside.

"Ye are worried," Torrian said as he passed them. "Sit down and we will explain."

Wulf said, "But ye dinnae have her, Cadyn. I was hoping ye would have brought her back."

Torrian repeated himself. "Give us the chance to explain. 'Tis a most complicated situation because we are dealing with two Englishmen."

Wulf cursed under his breath. "I'm sick with worry because I know of what our father is capable." He'd let go of Reyna and rubbed his leg as he spoke. "I had hoped this tragedy of betrothing her to a bastard would be over by now.

But our sire will no' let it go." Wulf let out a short bark at the sky. "Is my dear sister lost to me?"

Reyna said, "Dinnae jump to conclusions until ye hear everything."

Wulf nodded, stared at her, then tugged her down onto the spot next to him, wrapped his arms around her, and kissed her forehead before nodding to Torrian to explain. "What did I ever do without ye, Reyna?"

Once they were all settled, he asked, "Where is she? Tell me exactly what happened, please."

"She is back with her betrothed." Torrian sat in a large chair often saved for him.

Wulf barked a curse, dropping his leg to the floor and attempting to stand before falling back on the bench again. "What the hell happened?"

Cadyn explained, "She left the abbey for yer Aunt Canny's on her own, sneaking out in the night ahead of me. We'd made plans to leave but she decided to leave earlier. Fortunately, I heard her and was only a short distance behind her. We traveled together to Berwick when we ran into my sire and our chieftain." He motioned for Torrian to take over the telling of the tale.

Torrian said, "Yer sire happened. When we met up with Tryana, she asked us to escort her to yer aunt and uncle's because she believed it was important to warn them about yer sire."

"And because she wanted to retrieve yer mother's Bible."

"Aye. So we agreed to escort her with our two score guards, and I did not expect to find anyone else there. 'Twas my plan to get there, retrieve her Bible, then leave, but it didnae happen that way. Yer father was also there when we arrived. Apparently, he used trickery on her, stopping at the abbey to make her believe he was returning with the baron to retrieve her. She ran exactly as he expected so he was waiting for her. Your sire produced a writ signed by King Edward declaring Tryana's betrothal intact because coin had already been exchanged and the agreement between two noblemen was final."

"So return it," Wulf said. "I'll pay it if my sire willnae. He has a wicked gambling issue, so instead of paying for Tryana's wedding as any good sire should do, he was selling her instead. He found a buyer in the baron who lost his first wife and is desperate for heirs."

"Since it was no' the only thing mentioned in the writ, then I would guess it won't gain the result ye are hoping for. I dinnae think that was a choice in yer sire's mind because the baron still staked his claim on her. Yer father has taken his coin and wishes to be rid of yer sister. 'Twas an inconvenience for him to have to chase her down. 'Twas clear on his face that he resented this entire intrusion in his life." Torrian leaned back in the large chair, his arms crossed in front of him.

"Why did she no' listen to me and stay at the abbey? What the hell was she thinking?" He turned his head to face Cadyn. "Why did ye leave the abbey, Cadyn?" Wulf asked, stopping to plant his fists on the table as he glared at Cadyn. "Ye should have stopped her."

"Dinnae speak to my son in such a manner.

He's defended yer sister's honor throughout this daft situation." Cadyn was surprised to see his sire so upset at Wulf's words, but he was right.

Cadyn said, "'Tis fine, Papa. I'll answer." He turned his attention back to Wulf. "The baron came to the abbey first, but my arrows over his head convinced him to leave. Later, yer sire nearly broke the door of the abbey down, but since he was alone, he couldn't do much. He promised Tryana that he would be returning with the baron and a number of his guards the next day. As soon as he took his leave, Tryana made the decision to travel back to Scotland because she wished to be ahead of yer father. She was convinced she had time to get to yer uncle's house before yer sire returned. And she was truly upset by the effect yer sire's visit was having on the nuns. Sister Eda was visibly shaken, and Tryana didn't wish to be the cause of any more trouble."

"But the bastard beat her to Lowrans's house, of course. She is too innocent to suspect such treachery. 'Twas his plan all along."

"I warned her of that," Cadyn added. "I believe 'twas the reason why she left early. Since it would be just the two of us traveling together, I told her I would take her directly to Ramsay land. She begged me to stop at yer aunt and uncle's home. I advised against it, but once we came upon the Ramsay contingent, she asked our chief to take her there. She was frantic with worry about yer relatives. Apparently yer sire is cruel to others besides his bairns."

"And the baron was with him, ye say. How

many guards?" Wulf's face was much paler than it should have been. Cadyn didn't know exactly how to read into his actions.

"Five," Torrian answered. "All behind the next house eating and ignoring us. Enough to protect her through the Borderlands and get her back to York. He was not going to give up, but I think ye know that already. Am I correct, Wulf? Yer sire doesnae appear to be the kind to accept a rejection of one of his requests."

"True. My apologies, Cadyn. I'm sure ye did the best ye could do. Ye got her to Uncle Lowran's without any problem, and I feared she'd never make it once Dyna had told me the two of ye had left two days ago. What to do now? Any ideas?" Wulf looked defeated, and Cadyn felt the same way.

"Chief? What say ye?" Cadyn asked Torrian.

Torrian thought for a moment, then said, "We promised her someone would come for her within a sennight. I wouldn't wait that long for fear of an early marriage. We can take our leave whenever ye are ready, but I do believe she needs a family member like ye to get her out of this agreement. With a writ, it will take an important family member to refuse it. Ye are the only one to do that, Wulf. Yer sire went in the opposite direction, heading north, though he didnae say why. Ye will wish to steal her away from the baron as soon as ye can. With yer sire far away, ye are her best chance. Dinnae lose that opportunity."

Wulf sighed and ran his hands through his dark hair, staring up at the beams in the ceiling.

Cadyn knew exactly how he felt because he was more than ready to go dash after Tryana. He hated to admit to anyone that being so close to her had brought on some feelings that surprised him. He felt a fierce need to protect Tryana. Tension and frustration had been building in him since Tryana left with the baron, and now Cadyn was keeping a tight grip on his self-control to continue following his chief's plan rather than rushing to rescue her from the man who had hurt her before and whom she feared the most.

Wulf finally said, "All right, we shall plan to leave in two hours. Will that suit everyone?

"Nay," Reyna said. "Ye need one more day before ye will be able to get on a horse. Trust me, I know. Ye would never make it if we left now. Let Aunt Brenna tend yer wound and we'll be ready to go at first light."

He grumbled a bit, but gave in. "Fine. It seems I need to get my leg tended to first by Lady Brenna. Then we will go after her. We take enough guards so we dinnae have to fight to get her out. The number alone should convince the baron that we will not leave without her."

"And if there is a fight?" Cailean asked. "Are ye willing to fight for her, Chief?"

"Aye, whatever it takes," Torrian stated. "She cannae be held against her will. It goes against everything we stand for in Clan Ramsay."

Cadyn nearly let out a sigh of relief.

They'd be leaving soon. And a strange feeling of happiness erupted inside him.

What the hell did that mean?

CHAPTER SEVEN

TRYANA HAD THE sudden urge to heave all over the old carpet in her chamber. "But where are we going? And why now?" It was only a day after she'd returned from Scotland and everything was changing.

The sudden twist in her belly came from the realization that the baron and her father had probably connived even more. Still angry that her sire had used trickery to get her out of the abbey, she had to be quicker than he was to come up with a way out of this mess. Cadyn and his chieftain had promised to come for her, but they expected to find her in York. Yet the baron was now planning to take her to a place where no one would be able to find her, if she were to guess. Wales? London? She had no idea what the baron had planned. If she didn't stand up to him, she'd be married with no recourse because no one would be able to find her in time.

They only had a sennight to rescue her, and the possibility of that happening had just changed dramatically. They would have no idea where she was, would probably never find her until it was too late.

Until she became the Baroness of Topcliffe, the wife of Gareth Ward.

Until she had no recourse. And that upset her belly more than anything.

Thinking like her sire, she knew exactly what they'd planned. They were taking her to a place well hidden, outside of York. Perhaps outside of England. Across the water?

Forcing herself to keep control, she had to find a way out of this so she could return to Scotland. She'd planned to wait until Cadyn returned, then travel to Lochluin Abbey, but if the baron forced her to leave now, neither Wulf nor Cadyn would ever find her.

She had a sick feeling in the deepest pit of her belly.

Perhaps he was taking her straight to a kirk to be married. The baron stood in her doorway. "We go because I said so. That is all you need to know. Women do not have the right to question my actions. Your desires do not matter. Get ready now."

She squared her shoulders and spoke quietly, thinking about all she could lose. "Nay." She meant it to come out a bit more forceful, but bloodied knees reminded her of her possible penance.

He came closer, his face in a fury. "What did you say? Did you directly disobey me?"

She lifted her chin a notch because she did

have a right to know where she was being taken. "I say nay. My family believes..."

The baron's hand swung back in a wide arc and struck her hard across the cheek, throwing her backward and nearly losing her balance, but she stayed strong and would finish her words. "As your future wife, I have the right to know where I'll be living." She had more to say, but he never gave her the chance.

He slapped her again, but as soon as she finished her sentence, the next blow was a fist. All she saw was darkness as she braced her hands to catch her fall.

When she came to, she was lying on a cold, hard surface, but the familiar sway of being in motion made her realize she was traveling on the road in a cart. To where? The first thing she noticed was the immense pain in her head and the throbbing of her cheek. Dried blood dotted her face. She gingerly touched it, trying to scrape the blood away, but it was too sore to continue.

"Let it go," Bess said, sitting in the cart next to her. "And do be quiet. You must heal before you go against him again."

She tried to sit up but found that she was restrained, her hands bound in front of her. Panic set in as she tried to remember what had happened.

Then she heard his voice. He was speaking to someone, but she couldn't make out what he was saying. She strained to listen, hoping to get some clue as to where she was and what was going to happen to her.

"I don't care what it takes," he said, his voice low and menacing. "I need her to do what I want, when I want. She needs to learn her place."

Her heart sank as she realized what was happening. He was going to break her, to make her submit to his every desire. She had heard of men like him, but never thought she would be subject to such cruelty.

Another voice she didn't recognize replied, "I will assist you in any way I can. But you must remember that we are no longer in York, so do keep that in mind. Before long, we could run into the wild men of the north." The serious tone then switched to a lighter one as the baron jested on about the savage Highlanders he had met. That didn't matter to her. She had to learn their destination.

The men cajoled to each other about their journey, but she wasn't able to determine where they were headed. She looked at Bess and mouthed the word, "Where?"

Bess shrugged her shoulders, then gave her water to drink, which she accepted gladly. Perhaps she'd sit and keep her tongue for now. She had no idea where they were so she couldn't know which way to go if she escaped, especially with her hands bound together.

Perhaps she'd get the chance to run when she had to see to her needs. She folded her hands in her lap and kept a close eye on the landscape as they passed.

In the dark, it all looked much the same. One forest blended into another. One glen, one knoll.

They all looked the same. Of all things to do, it wasn't wise of her to put herself at risk before they left simply because she needed to know which way they had headed.

Bess probably didn't know much about the different towns, cities, even countries. She had a family, so she hoped they wouldn't be taken too far away. "But your family, Bess?"

"I know. He told me we would return in less than a moon, and he would pay me extra. I will mind my tongue until then. You should too since you've seen what he is capable of. Please do not antagonize him anymore."

"But I need to know where we are going. London? The Borderlands? Where?"

"Cease your chatter," one of the guards said. "Our lord said for ye to be quiet. We do not need to attract any men looking for a lady to spend the night with."

Tryana cursed inwardly. All she could do was hope that they'd be allowed the chance to see to their needs eventually. It would be the best time to attempt to escape, run for all she was worth and find a place to hide until they gave up.

But she didn't like the fact that she had no idea where they were. If they were headed to London, she'd need to head north. If they were going to the Borderlands, she'd need to head north also. She could try her aunt and uncle's house, but it would be the first place the bastard would look for her.

She needed a different solution. If she had the chance, she would run. Run and head north. No matter where she was, she'd have to head north to get to anywhere she would be safe. The only places that she knew to be safe were Ramsay land, wherever that was, or to Lochluin Abbey. She knew someone there who would help her.

Ramsay land was in Scotland as was Lochluin Abbey, so heading north was the safest guess. How was she going to do it? She had a mantle and it was late summer, still warm enough. But she hadn't been into the Highlands for a long time. How cold did it get there?

If she were to guess, Ramsay land would be in the Highlands also. But how far and which way to go, she had no idea. But if she asked, someone would surely know where Clan Ramsay was, wouldn't they?

Or perhaps Wulf was looking for her. And she could run into Cadyn's group as well. It wouldn't be that difficult.

She just had to make her move. Her decision made, she'd be on her way as soon as they stopped. Once she was free, she would head north for Ramsay land and hope Cadyn was still there. He would protect her if the baron followed her, but if she were to wager, she'd wager against the baron. In favor of Cadyn MacAdam.

First, she'd say ten prayers for her safety.

And for a guiding hand to direct her to Ramsay Castle, then she'd move on to Lochluin Abbey. The most important person in her life was there. He just didn't know it yet.

CHAPTER EIGHT

THE NIGHT BEFORE they were to leave, Cadyn paced up in the parapets. It was a clear spot, and he could see what happened around Ramsay Castle. He ran his hands through his hair because his mind was taking him to odd places, and he didn't know what was right. He'd gone over and over their plan, the number of guards they'd take, the path they would follow to York. He'd spoken with Wulf about their father, to see if there was anything else about Wrath de Gray that could help them decide how to handle this ridiculous situation.

A cruel baron wished to marry an innocent lass against her wishes. How fortunate Cadyn was to have been born as a lad.

The door opened and his grandsire stepped out, closing the door with the usual bang, something that always put a smirk on Cadyn's face. He thought the man's penchant to slam doors was entertaining and he'd tried at a younger age to copy him, but it just couldn't be done right.

It was true what so many had often said. There was only one Logan Ramsay.

"Grandsire, how do ye fare?"

"I'm well, Cadyn. I'm proud of the way ye protected the lass. It seems ye did a fine job, but what are yer plans now?" He leaned over the parapets, taking a deep breath of the clear air. The castle was only on the edge of the Highlands but the beauty of the surrounding forests was indescribable. "Though I can see ye are a wee bit unsettled."

"Aye, I wished to go after her this day."

His grandsire shook his head. "Reyna was correct. Ye canno' go when Wulf would slow ye down. Ye need him there. She made the correct decision. Ye have a sennight."

"If the baron is being truthful," he grumbled, something he doubted.

"The church willnae marry them in less time. Ye know that. There was a date that was a fortnight away. If they move it up to a sennight, I'd be surprised. Definitely not on the morrow. And ye know Wulf could burn with the fever again and we could lose him."

Cadyn hadn't considered that thought. "Not with Aunt Brenna."

"Correct, not if he were here. But if he runs off without a care, ignores Reyna's words to use the poultice, to drink the potions, he could easily go back into the fever. The dusty road is no' kind to wounds. You can believe someone who has been on the road many times."

Cadyn grinned. "Did it no' happen to ye once, Grandsire? Does Da no' talk about the time he had to lift ye up and put ye on yer horse? And ye rode with him?"

"Aye, he does. Young and foolish. I was badly beaten but I was still stubborn. Nearly killed me. If Cailean and Gavin had no' been there, I probably would have died. So listen to this old man. Ye go on the morrow. Let him have a good night's rest. I always believed in sleep. So what exactly is yer plan once ye leave here?" He crossed his arms and leaned against the back wall.

"I'm no' sure."

"Why no'?" He pushed back enough to stare at his grandson, that look that Cadyn knew could assess a person so well, he would probably know what time you last ate and what your favorite color was from one glance. How he wished to learn that special skill.

"I'll agree with the plan, to leave on the morrow, that we shouldnae wait for long, but I'm no' sure how we shall get her out." He glanced over at the man he admired so, noticing that even though he was gray-haired and bearded, the eyes were still as alert as ever. There was no denying his craftiness.

His grandfather's eyes bored into his and he stood his ground, knowing the man was about to pull something from him that he might not even know was there.

"Ye dinnae agree with Wulf. Why no'?"

"Hellfire, Grandda! I'm no' even sure what I think. How can ye know?"

The Logan grin crossed his face and he waggled his brow at him. "Because ye are much like me.

'Tis just like looking at myself many years ago. No' so hard to think like ye. Ye dinnae think she is in York, and I also caught that ye will follow her wherever she is. Out with yer truth."

Cadyn blushed and leaned on the cold stone again, staring out across the trees. He couldn't hide his scowl for being caught so well. "Hell. I dinnae think she is even in England. I think she's in the Highlands."

"What makes ye think so?"

"I had a dream." He paused, ruminating about how much he dared to tell the crafty man. "I saw her in a tower somewhere calling out for me. I fell asleep on the ground on the way back from York, and she appeared to me."

"So how do ye know she's in the Highlands? The tower could be in England or Wales."

He shrugged. "I know, but I dinnae know how to explain it. I just have a feeling. And there were mountains behind the towers. I recall them well."

"We need Molly or Dyna."

That comment caught him more than any other. That meant his grandfather believed what he said, or at least might consider some truth there. "Do ye think they could tell?" He glanced over at his grandsire, who was now staring over the landscape.

"Mayhap. 'Tis possible. And ye will go to the Highlands no matter where Wulf goes, will ye no'? Ye will follow yer gut and chase after a lass ye barely know?" This time, the old man didn't look at him, giving him the chance to consider his response carefully.

"Aye, I will follow my gut, just like ye did, Grandda."

"And she's the one?"

"I dinnae know, but I'd like to find out." That was the most honest answer he could give the man.

"Well then, ye better hope all that rustling I hear is Dyna or Molly coming for a visit." He tipped his head to the west of them. "See that, coming down the path could be the reason ye needed to wait until the morrow to take yer leave."

Cadyn had been thinking so hard, he hadn't noticed.

"I canno' see as ye can anymore, lad. Who is on our land?" He tipped his head in the direction of the visitors.

Cadyn leaned over the parapets, squinting into the moonlit night. "I see a Grant plaid."

"How many?"

"Mayhap half a score or more." He couldn't make out any faces in the dark.

"'Tis the Bruce contingency. Something has happened to bring them from Berwick. This is their resting spot." Grandda opened the door, but then stopped to clasp his shoulder. "Mayhap ye are right about Tryana being in Scotland. Time to greet the travelers."

"I'm happy to greet them."

"Oh, and one more thing, lad," Grandda said, blocking his passage through the doorway. "If ye tell yer sire what I just said, ye will regret it." Then he grinned and pushed him through the door.

They'd spent the night in a stable, though Tryana had no idea where it was located. They could be in Wales for all she knew. Much as she'd hoped to escape already, the opportunity hadn't arisen yet. Determined to escape, as soon as she had the chance on the morrow, she would run. At present, the stable was manned by guards on both ends. This was an impossible situation. She decided to accept it and try to get the best sleep she could.

Fortunately, the baron kept his distance, spending most of his time whispering with his guards at the opposite end of the stable. She looked for any clues of their location, but she found nothing. They were fed dried meat and bread. Tryana saved some of the dried meat and stuffed it in her linen square. She would get free on the morrow. She had to. With that thought, she fell asleep, dreaming of green eyes and a handsome blond guard.

They were awakened at first light, given a small basin of water to wash up with, and a bucket to use inside the stable.

There'd be no escape until they were on the road. She noticed a small dagger on the shelf on her way out, so she carefully grabbed it and hid it inside a fold in her gown. This day would be her freedom. She had to be alert.

Impatient as she was, she never had the opportunity to run until nearly the end of the day.

The group stopped for a moment to take care of their needs. Tryana didn't care where they were. They'd been traveling for two days and this was the first chance she had to escape. "Bess, cover for me. I'm running away."

Bess's eyes widened. "But if he catches you, he may kill you."

"Then I guess I'll have to run faster."

The baron said, "Take them over there and stand guard. Untie their hands until they finish, then tie them up again. Keep an eye on her, Bess. Just scream if anything happens." Then he made his way in the opposite direction to the edge of the forest where all the men headed.

This was her chance. She spoke kindly to the guard. "We'll only be a few moments."

He nodded and turned his back to them.

She moved back to a spot behind a tree, rustled enough to make the man think she was taking care of her needs, but then strode steadily in the opposite direction. It wasn't quite dark yet so she was able to see well enough. She tiptoed through the bushes until she found a path, one that went in the opposite direction.

She took off in a dead run, praying she would get far enough away to hide somewhere before the men came for her. Tryana ran and ran until she heard the crash of bushes behind her.

Glancing back over her shoulder, to her delight she saw Bess running straight toward her. "Go faster. I think they've discovered us."

"Why, Bess?"

"Because I was supposed to watch over you. I do not want a beating either. Now run!"

The two ran until Tryana thought her lungs would burst. She crossed over a stream, happy to see there were stones to keep her boots from getting wet, but she didn't know how much longer they could run.

They eventually found themselves at the outskirts of a forest and stepping into a vast clearing, the sound of water not far. Tryana panted heavily, her chest heaving with each breath. Bess, on the other hand, seemed to have no trouble keeping up with her. They slowed their pace and stopped to catch their breath.

Tryana looked around. They were surrounded by tall trees, their leaves rustling in the wind. The sun was setting, casting a warm, golden glow on everything around them. It was beautiful, but the danger was still lurking around them.

"We need to find a place to hide," Bess said, her voice laced with urgency. "We can't stay out here for long. They'll be along behind us soon."

Tryana nodded. She glanced around once more before spotting a small waterfall on the edge of the forest. "Over there," she said, pointing towards it.

Bess followed her gaze and nodded. "Perfect, now go."

Together, they made their way to the waterfall, the heavy rock arrangements around it abounding with hiding places. She climbed up the small hill toward the waterfall, being careful not to lose her footing and fall backward.

Once she saw Bess made it safely behind her, she spun around, totally surprised to run into someone, knocking him down as she tumbled over him.

It was a young lad. "Hellfire, I'm trying to save ye, lady, no' kill ye."

She sat up, Bess now behind her. "Who are you?" The lad had long dark hair curling at the nape of his neck.

The cheeky boy yanked out a small sword from his sheath. "I'm the one who will save ye from all those men chasing ye. Follow me."

She bolted to her feet and whispered, "Come, Bess. We found our savior."

The two followed the lad who looked to be about seven or eight summers. "Laddie, where are we going? Do you know or are you just guessing or playing out in the forest? Do you live nearby?"

Tryana glanced around, but she hadn't seen any huts or cottages along the way. He ignored her, moving stealthily through the brush as if he'd lived here his entire life. But eventually, she needed more information, so she grabbed his shoulder. "Where are you taking us? How much farther? We could hide near that waterfall. Have you not considered that?"

He spun around with a scowl. "Right up here to the hidden cave *behind* the waterfall." He pointed and said, "Ye should be more trusting, lady."

At this point, she didn't have much choice. She could see Bess was limping, and Tryana could feel branches and twigs snagging on the fabric at her back as she ducked through the trees and brush.

Brushing the bugs away from her face, swatting at the midges who seemed to find their way up her legs, she hoped they would reach the cave quickly. Then she heard the bellow of a man a distance away.

The baron.

"Hurry." The sound came out without much thought, but they had to go faster.

She closed her mouth and pushed the boy along, grabbing onto Bess's hand to make sure she kept up. The lad proudly led them up to the waterfall which was much larger than she would have guessed when looking up at it from the clearing below.

She held her breath as she neared the waterfall, the water hitting the stone at the base so hard that a smoky mist hovered around it. "See, they'll never see the cave behind this and besides, my friend guards this and he'll scare everyone away."

"What friend?"

"Behind that big rock. 'Tis my friend Thor."

"Thor?"

She nearly went in that direction, but the lad said, "Nay, lady. Ye'll no' like Thor."

Sticking her head behind the rock, she had to bite her tongue to keep from screaming at the big face that jumped up to stare at her. She turned quickly to Bess and said, "Do not look."

"He's just an otter, lady. He willnae hurt ye if ye leave him alone. Bye, Thor. Guard us well."

The lad moved on and seemed to disappear, but she followed him, ducking as they went behind the water, the falls acting like a curtain across the large stone cave in the back. She had to admit, she would never have dared to enter the cave alone. What had she been thinking?

Once inside, he said, "Follow me to the back. It goes through this dark spot, then there's a hidden bend and then ye come to my house."

"Your house?" Each step as timid as the next, her vision darting from the cobwebs overhead to the sudden intense fear of bats overcoming her. If this lad was strong enough, she surely was.

A voice called out to her. "I know you are in there, Bess and Tryana. We are coming in."

She followed the boy until she thought there was nowhere else to go. The lad disappeared and she stood in the dark, Bess huddled next to her, neither knowing where to go. A hand darted out and grabbed her.

She walked straight into a wall.

Disoriented, Tryana stumbled back, her heart racing with fear. Her hands fumbled in the dark, searching for something, anything to hold onto. Her fingers grazed a rough stone surface, and she palpated with her fingertips until she found a deep crevice. She pulled herself into it, Bess following close behind. She bumped right into the lad, who whispered, "Dinnae step on me. 'Tis plenty of room for all of us."

The sound of footsteps grew louder, and Tryana held her breath, praying they wouldn't be found. She heard a gruff voice cursing outside the cave, and a shiver ran down her spine. She had never felt so vulnerable in her life.

The footsteps faded away, and Tryana let out

a sigh of relief. She turned to the boy, her eyes adjusting to the darkness. "Thank you," she said, her voice barely above a whisper. "I don't know what we would have done without you."

The boy shrugged. "'Tis naught. I've been hiding out here for a while now. 'Tis not safe for anyone to be in the woods alone. Ye need me. I'm yer protector now. Just like Thor."

Who was this cheeky lad?

CHAPTER NINE

CADYN RAN OUT the door, leaving his grandfather seated by the hearth, waving him on. He rushed to the stables, excited to see who exactly was here. As he passed Reyna and Wulf in the great hall, he called over his shoulder to Reyna, "Visitors have arrived. I'll bring them inside." Wulf wasn't moving yet as he should be, but he was improving.

Gavin came along behind him. "Is my daughter one of them?"

"I dinnae know yet." He knew his aunt and uncle were worried about Ysenda, though they needn't be. She had an eye nearly as good as Reyna.

The first person he noticed out by the stable was Maitland, who waved at him. "Hope ye have some dinner for us yet, Cadyn. We're all hungry."

"Tell me quickly why ye are here, then I'll go speak with Mama and Merewen. They'll see ye are all fed."

Maitland handed the reins of his horse over to the stable lad, then moved over to speak with Cadyn while the others followed. "We're all here.

The garrison left Berwick so our king sent a message for us to follow the garrisons. Two of them are headed into Scotland. They'll not be hard to catch because they travel so slowly. Dyna and I decided 'twould be best to meet here and make our plans. Get a good meal and a sound night's sleep, then we'll separate into two groups on the morrow."

"A sound plan in my eyes." He was ecstatic because now he could speak with Dyna and be involved in their next plan. Surveying the group, he counted: Maitland, Dyna, Isla and Grif, Lewis, Ysenda, Thea, Alaric, Ceit, Tevis, and Dobbin.

He spun around and headed inside to alert his mother and Merewen, opening the door and heading into the great hall with a shout to Reyna and Wulf. "They're all here for the night. Garrisons are on the move."

His father had come down the stairs behind his mother. Cadyn called out to her, "Mama, is there enough food for eleven more? The patrol is here."

His mother replied, "'Tis plenty of stew if ye are no' eating again. The pot is full and still cooking. Cook added more vegetables."

Cadyn frowned and said, "I'll eat bread. Cook had many loaves already baked." He knew he was known for his appetite, but with all his worries, he wasn't thinking much on food, instead worried about Tryana.

Grandsire came along and said, "MacAdam, I think yer son is in love. Either that or he's sickly. There must be something wrong if he's not overly concerned about what he's eating."

His father gave him an odd look but said, "We'll need more ale, Cadyn."

He scowled at his grandfather but strode to the cellar stairs to go to the buttery. They would need lots of ale and mead. They could be talking well into the middle of the night.

He'd not miss any of it. Heading into the cellar, he did his best to overhear all the conversations. His grandda yelled, "Sorcha, find yer mother. And see if we have enough fruit for the travelers. Yer son will eat anything that is set out, so ye must have more." Cadyn rolled his eyes at this comment. He knew it to be true, but he hated that others shared in that knowledge.

Torrian came in from the tower and greeted the group. "Eat, then we can talk about the issues. I wish to get ye all settled. I believe a storm is brewing outside, so we'll find room for ye all inside. We have plenty of chambers and enough pallets for the hall, if necessary. Kyle is settling the horses, then he'll be in."

It took about half the hour to get everyone settled and get the food out. But as often happens, those on patrol eat so quickly that they finished in a snap. Maitland clasped his belly and said, "Ramsay, ye always have the best cook. So good to have warm food with some flavoring. Many thanks to ye. The stew was excellent, especially with the beans."

Wulf had waited patiently, or impatiently if anyone watched how often he twirled Reyna's hair around his finger. Finally he asked, "Any word on my sister?"

The group quieted and Maitland replied, "I had two follow the baron's group and they headed straight to York. She was with them when they arrived. We have not been back since then."

"So tell us more about the track of the English garrisons," Cadyn said, watching as his grandda now stood up and paced. Cadyn had a difficult time not doing the same.

"The garrison left Berwick. They headed into England, but another garrison has been seen heading to the Borderlands. We also received word that a garrison has been seen in the Lowlands. We arenae sure exactly what is taking place, but our king has asked us to investigate all English garrisons, but not to engage without gathering more forces. We are strictly on a mission to follow and report."

"How many garrisons?" Uncle Gavin asked, taking a seat across from Merewen and Ysenda.

Dyna said, "We think three, though we know not the purpose of any of them. And there may be only two headed into Scotland."

Torrian said, "They could be headed to any number of castles for takeover. Edward wishes to have control over all our castles. He'd go as far into Ayrshire and Perthshire if he thought he could control a castle."

Uncle Gavin said, "But they'd be surrounded by Scots. All the clans have many allies. Only a few side with Edward. They'd be sitting ducks at any of the castles."

Several minutes of smaller conversations took place while his grandfather paced. Cadyn listened to them all, but he made his way to Wulf and Reyna. "Your thoughts, de Gray?"

"I think she's in York, and I'm headed there on the morrow as long as the storm allows us. Join us?" His arm stayed around Reyna, Cadyn noticed. Their interest in each other hadn't waned at all. If anything, the two were closer than ever, but Wulf was tense. The issue surrounding Tryana and their father would not leave him until Tryana was safe.

Cadyn felt the same. "I'm no' sure. I have this odd feeling that she is no longer in York." He made his statement, then observed Wulf to gauge his reaction to Cadyn's declaration.

"She's in York with the baron. He'll no' let go of her. 'Tis where we go first." He ran the back of his fingers across the beard stubble on his face. "But just in case she is no', where do ye think she is, Cadyn?"

"I wish I knew for certes."

"Well, we surely cannae cover all of England while we are searching for her. We dinnae have enough men. I think we head to York and if they are no' there, I'm sure we can get information from one of their remaining guards. They were seen in York so 'tis the best place to start."

Dyna called out to him. "Cadyn, may I speak with ye, please?"

Someone else called out to Wulf, so there was no reaction on Wulf's part to Dyna's request. Reyna kept her eye on them though. His cousin didn't miss much.

Dyna led him over to two chairs near the

hearth, away from the large group at the trestle tables. "Cadyn, I know ye are close with Tryana. I'm surprised to say this because I rarely have dreams about people I'm not close with, but she appeared in a dream to me. Even though we are no' close, sometimes I will have visions of people who are truly in trouble. I have no' decided yet how it comes about but..."

"Does no' matter to me how it comes about, Dyna. Please tell me because I had a dream about her too." Cadyn hated to interrupt her but he was anxious to see if there were any similarities between their dreams. Tryana was definitely in trouble, and it wasn't in York.

"Ye did? I didnae know ye were a seer."

"I am no'. Or I never have been before. Please continue," he prodded.

Dyna nodded. "Tryana is in trouble and she's no' in York."

He stared at her wide-eyed, moving to the edge of his seat. "'Tis the same dream I've had. She's no' in York. Where is she in yer dream?"

Dyna smiled. "Aye, she's in the Highlands."

He bolted out of his seat, swinging his arms wide. "Aye, exactly the same. I had a dream that she is in trouble in the Highlands." He spun around to call out to Wulf. "Wulf, ye must hear this."

Wulf limped over along with Reyna, Maitland, and his grandsire. "What has ye so excited?" Grandda asked.

"Dyna and I had the same dream. Tryana is no' in York. She's in the Highlands."

Wulf studied one face, then the other. "Ye both had the same dream? Are ye a seer, Cadyn? I've heard of Dyna's reputation, but no' yers."

"Nay, I've never been until now, but I'm telling ye. Tryana is in the Highlands. We had the same dream so it must be true. Do ye no' agree, Grandda?" He knew the man would agree with him. He has believed in seers all his life.

Grandda lifted his chin. "'Tis possible, for certes."

"'Tis no' enough information. The Highlands is quite an expanse, or have ye forgotten," Wulf drawled. "Where in the Highlands is she? The exact location?"

Cadyn was so sure they were right that he said, "She's in a tower. In a large castle."

Dyna spoke almost at the exact same time. "She's near a waterfall."

Cadyn's shoulders fell. "What? Near a waterfall? Nay, she's in a large castle with two towers and she's in one of them."

Dyna shook her head. "She's near a waterfall hiding in a cave."

Wulf slapped his face with both hands. "Hellfire." Then he limped back to the table.

Grandda said, "Unless there is a tower with a waterfall next to it, I think ye two have a problem."

Cadyn fell back into his chair. Where would they go now?

CHAPTER TEN

"IN HERE," THE lad whispered, pulling her into a large open cave with a hole in the stone above them, letting enough light in to see the entire cave. She put a finger to his mouth because someone was behind them.

A different voice said, "They came this way."

"But they could have left on the other side of the waterfall. It is plenty wide enough to hide behind, and we would never have seen them if they were at that end."

The first voice said, "We'll go that way." The two departed.

Bess squeezed her hand, but she said nothing. The three ducked up against the wall of the cave, hoping they couldn't be seen, but she was quite sure they'd never guess there was an opening where the boy had tugged her through. They just had to be quiet until the two left.

It was amazingly simple and safe.

They waited about ten minutes when a voice said, "I checked over there. They did not come this way. Caves can be deceiving. Go back out.

They probably climbed to the top of the waterfall. There's an open meadow not far."

A different voice said, "Once I thought someone was in the back of a cave but it was the echo. The person was actually on a higher vantage point across from the cave. It was quite strange, but truly deceiving. They could be across from us. We'll check both places."

The sound of retreating footsteps caused her to let out the breath she'd been holding. She gazed around the cave, surprisingly warm and cozy. There were three flat rocks in various spots and a pile of tools in the corner.

Tryana sat down on the closest rock, Bess doing the same on the next one. "Lad, you saved us. Many thanks to you. Who are you? And why do you live here?"

"I dinnae live here. I just decided I needed to search for my sire. I've no' seen him in a long while, and I miss him. I'm allowed to visit here for a wee bit."

Tryana had the odd feeling that things were not exactly as the boy said. "What is your name?"

"My name?" He paused for just a bit. "Magni."

"Magni? The son of Thor?"

"Aye, 'tis me. I'm the son of Thor."

"But is the otter not named Thor?" Bess asked.

"Aye, but I named him after my da and my da is Thor." Magni's bottom lip came out in a big pout.

Tryana knew he was giving her a false name, because the pause was a bit too long. No one hesitated to give their name, but she decided to go along with him for now. "How many summers are ye, Magni?"

"Almost eight summers, but I'm a good fighter. I've trained with my sire's men in archery." He moved over to the side where all the tools were and pulled out a small bow and appropriately sized arrows. "See, I hunt with these."

She noticed the makings of a small fire under the shaft of light, bones tossed about. "Did you make the fire? Cook your own meat?"

"Aye. I caught a rabbit and he was a fat one. What is yer name?"

"Tryana, and this is Bess."

"Ladylana and Bess."

"Nay, Tryana."

"'Tis what I said, Ladylana."

She decided that Lady Lana was close enough, even though he mashed it together to be one long word.

"How long have you been here, lad?" Bess asked, removing the bag she had over her shoulder.

"A fortnight or more, surely that long at least." He didn't say much else, but she noticed he had his own bag in the corner also. If she were to guess, he'd only been here a night or two. There were only enough bones for one rabbit. There was a plaid and a blanket though she didn't recognize the colors in the plaid. They appeared to be a dark brown with a hint of green among the dirt.

Bess opened her sack and said, "Here, my lady. I grabbed a few things before we left. Here are some trews and another gown for you. I have trews for myself. We cannot stay in gowns out here in the wild. The midges are terrible, so put them on. Oh, and I also threw in some apples and some dried meat."

"You thought we would be running away, Bess?"

"Nay. The baron barely feeds his help. I'm always hungry, and the trews are for sleeping at night. My legs get cold, but now I'm glad I brought them because I need them for the cave. I saw the apples so I took them. Here is one for you and one for me. Magni, would you like one?"

"Aye," he said, rushing over to grab the sweet treat. "Many thanks, Bess. I found one tree with fruit but I could no' climb it. I go back every day looking for any windfalls. I love apples but they are too high for me."

The three sat in a circle, chomping noisily on what was likely to be all they had for their evening meal, though she suddenly recalled she had dried meat so they shared that too. Tryana didn't care if she ate much. She was grateful to be well hidden where she was. What she needed to do was plan from here. For one thing, she still had no idea whether they were in Scotland or England. But her ultimate goal was to find Wulf or Cadyn, then find her way to the abbey.

"Magni, where are we?"

He got a twisted look on his face and drawled, "In a cave." Then he giggled at his jest.

She narrowed her gaze at him and he giggled, a sound that delighted her, making her smile, the small act reminding her of simpler times in her life. "Magni, we left from York in England two days ago. I was knocked out. I do not know what direction we went in. But you definitely have a Scottish sound to your tongue."

Bess shrugged her shoulders. "I'm terrible with directions. I have no idea where we are. Near London? Wales? Where are we, Magni? I left my family back in York. I must return someday."

"London? Wales? Ye are in Scotland, ladies."

Her heart soared with that revelation. "We are? I'm so pleased. How far into Scotland? Do you know how to get to Clan Ramsay? Or to Cameron land? Lochluin Abbey?" She could only hope to be near one of them. If they were close to Ramsay land, she could hope to find Wulf and have him take her to Lochluin Abbey. "My brother is on Ramsay land."

Though if he escorted her, she'd have to do some serious explaining once they arrived at the abbey and she searched out the person she was looking for.

In fact, it was a lad about Magni's age who she was looking for. "Have you ever been to Lochluin Abbey, Magni?" She held her breath, waiting for his answer. And wondered what she would say if he had been there.

"Nay, my sire is a Highland chieftain. I'm from way up north. But he went on patrol for a skirmish. I'm following him."

First Thor, now a chieftain. Poor Magni was living in a fantasy world.

She decided to let him believe whatever he wished to believe.

In the meantime, she needed rest. "Would you

be able to lead us to Ramsay land or Lochluin Abbey on the morrow? I'll let you know which one by then."

"Aye. I know how to get to Lochluin Abbey. 'Tis no' too far from here. I'm a terrific tracker too. My sire taught me how to track people so I'll make sure we are no' on the same path as those evil men who stole you away. Who are those men?" Magni got up and picked up a stone, tossing it against the wall to see where it would go. Sometimes he tried to catch it as if it would bounce.

"Cruel men who wish to make me marry an evil man."There were many days in her life when she'd done exactly what everyone else wished for her to do, but no more. "I'll not do it."

In fact, on the morrow she'd ask Magni to teach her how to fire that bow. She might need to shoot someone real soon.

Lochluin Abbey, learn to shoot a bow, find Wulf and Reyna.

She had goals and none of them had to do with an old baron.

CHAPTER ELEVEN

THE PATROL GROUP from Berwick had returned to Ramsay land with strict instructions. Cadyn waited to hear what the new information was and how this could affect his travels. He could use help in finding Tryana, especially Dyna's special talents. She was a seer and could help him find the lass. But the two leaders were presently discussing their new plans in the hall, deciding where to go next. Apparently, King Robert had been vague about their travels.

Maitland said, "If ye and Cadyn can agree on where in the Highlands we are going, then I could consider sending a patrol in that direction."

"What do ye think we should do?" Dyna asked, crossing her arms and tossing her long white plait over her shoulder. She had two smaller plaits on either side of her head.

"I think we split into two groups. One goes with Wulf to York. We have to follow that one through. Torrian gave the lass his word that he would send someone to travel to the baron's home in order to rescue her from the bastard."

Wulf said, "'Tis the group Reyna and I will go with. Decide who else, but we'll be going to York. Since I'm no' yet in the best shape to fight, I'd appreciate some guards with us, whether ye send any of our patrol along also 'tis up to ye."

Maitland paced next to the fire. "Then we send Isla, Grif, Lewis, Ysenda, and Thea with ye. Dyna, which way do ye wish to go?"

Dyna said, "To the Highlands with Cadyn. Ye know there is one garrison going in that direction so we must go too."

"Then Cadyn goes with ye, and ye both search for her once ye discover where the garrison is going," Grandda said.

"Nay, I am no' following an English garrison unless it proves to be the baron, but I doubt he has that many guards." Cadyn was not running over the mountains in the Highlands after a lone English garrison.

Cailean approached from the trestle table. "Cadyn, ye'll go where Maitland and Dyna send ye."

Grandda said, "For once ye are making some sense, MacAdam." Everyone had loved to tease Cailean about the fact that Logan did not think him strong enough to protect his family. He'd always taunted his father, even though his sire had jumped over the edge of a cliff just to save his mother.

His mother said it was all a show to put on for the others. That if Grandda hadn't trusted him, they never would have married. As Cadyn had grown older, the more he saw respect from his grandfather toward his father. But right now, he didn't wish to listen to either of them.

But he'd be forced into it probably.

Maitland said, "Logan, ask yer chief if we can send a half dozen guards with Wulf and Reyna to York. I think Dyna and I should start our groups out together, see if we can find the two garrisons. Once we know how many and where they are located, then we can decide whether or not to split. When we split, Cadyn can go with Dyna since they are both having dreams about where she is. Once we uncover the two groups, we'll split. English garrisons do not hide well in Scotland. We'll find them."

"Mayhap I'll go alone." Cadyn couldn't believe he'd actually said the words, but he was feeling stronger and stronger about his dream, though he didn't comprehend why Dyna's was different.

"The hell ye will," came two shouts in unison—his sire and his grandsire.

His grandfather said, "Go with Dyna. Follow her senses. Start as a large group and make decisions along the way. 'Tis the best plan for a patrol group, and 'tis all our king wants from ye at present."

Maitland stood next to Cadyn and clasped his shoulder. "Uncle Logan is right. Dyna and I will travel with ye, Tevis, Alaric, Ceit, and Dobbin. We need enough archers with us in case a garrison goes on the attack. We leave at first light."

Cadyn mumbled, "Agreed. But if we find the baron, I'm going after him."

Maitland said, "I promise if we split, ye and

Dyna can go after the baron or wherever ye think Tryana is."

Torrian said, "If either of ye need more men, just send a missive and I'll send however many ye need."

Cadyn nodded his head. This was going to be a long journey.

The group broke up, so Cadyn moved over to a trestle table where his parents and sister sat. Before long, a wee lass entered the hall with Lise and Liliana directly behind her. "Mama, I'm going to practice my bow now."

Cadyn's youngest sister of only five winters was named Lainey and she was a busy lass. "I am going to be Gwyneth when I practice this time." His sister liked to pretend to be someone else. Grandmama was one of her favorites.

"Lainey, say goodbye to Cadyn because he's leaving soon. And so is Ceit." Her mother busied herself, fussing over Lainey's golden plait.

"Ye are leaving again? But then I canno' play with ye." Her lips came out in a big pout, but her father scooped her up and tossed her high up in the air, setting her into giggles.

"Cailean, I was no' done fixing her plait," his mother said.

"But Mama, I like it when Papa tosses me in the air." Lainey giggled furiously when her father caught her and kissed her neck.

His father set her down and said, "Be a good lassie and do what Mama tells ye to do, sweeting."

"Nay, Gwyneth. My name is Gwyneth now." She lifted her bow and aimed at nothing in the corner. "Ceit will be the best warrior on the morrow." Then she ran over and hugged her sister, then her brother. "Godspeed, both of ye. And ye must promise to play targets when ye return."

"I promise." Cadyn would never argue with her, and she rarely forgot any promises.

Lainey would be a wee bit wild when she grew up, if he were to guess.

The next morn, Tryana opened her eyes, surprised to see the sun beaming down through the space in the rock above. The first thing she thought was they'd made it. She sat up and her gaze scanned the small enclosure. Bess was still sleeping, but Magni had disappeared.

She waited a few moments to see if he would return quickly, but he did not. Bess awakened and said, "We're still safe?"

"Aye. We have not been discovered yet, but I would like to find Magni. I have not seen him since I awakened. I'll go out and see if I see him." She stood, a bit stiffly from sleeping on stone, but she was hale and away from the baron. That was the important point.

"Promise me you'll not leave the cave, Tryana. I do not wish to be here alone."

"I promise. I'll only go as far as the waterfall. I'll peek about and see if I see him or signs of anyone else."

Bess nodded with a large yawn, stretching her legs.

"But I also would like you to promise me something, Bess."

The woman scowled and said, "Perhaps. What is it?"

"You must promise me that if we are followed again, if you have the chance, you will go back to York to your family. I do not want you trying to save me. The baron will make you pay for coming with me. If he manages to grab ahold of me, I wish for you to go the opposite way. All the way back to York without me."

"I promise."

"My thanks. I'll head outside to see if I can locate Magni." Tryana followed the path back out to the front of the cave. She was glad to see there were no alternate routes so it was impossible to get lost in the cave. Once the sound of the falls became so heavy she knew she was drawing close, she slowed her steps, praying that the baron would not be outside holding Magni hostage.

A loud scream carried to her and she saw a shadow pass over the waterfall. Was that Magni?

She ran out, ready to jump into the water and save him, but she just caught his leap into the water, landing with a huge splash. He came up with a spurt of water from his mouth and a giggle.

"Magni! What are you doing? You'll hurt yourself." Tryana was so sick with worry that she completely forgot about the possibility they'd be seen. "Did you jump from the top of the waterfall? Truly? That is too high!"

"Swimming. I needed a bath, Ladylana." He hopped out of the water onto the opposite bank without a stitch of clothing on and Tryana couldn't hide her shock, her eyes going straight to the gray clouds above.

"But you have nothing on." She turned around, refusing to look at him, though she peeked to watch him run up the side of the embankment toward the top of the waterfall. It wasn't the largest, so she chided herself to stop worrying. "A fish could bite you."

He chuckled as he hurried up the embankment, his bare bottom flashing white amongst the ferns and fronds of the lush landscape. "Nay, a fish could never catch me. I'm too fast."

Naked and unashamed, he stood on a stone at the top of the waterfall, arms totally outstretched before he jumped. "Watch me, Ladylana. I make a big splash."

"Be careful, Magni."

Bess came out behind her just as Magni launched himself far away from the waterfall, as carefree as ever with a huge smile on his face. He landed with a large plop, sending a spray of water straight at Tryana and hitting her in the face.

He surfaced with a sputter and a giggle. "'Twas the biggest yet."

"Magni, please pause for a moment. Have you seen anyone?"

He stopped after he climbed out of the water, shivering a bit as a breeze caught him. "Nay, no one." He raced back up the incline to the top of the waterfall. "Watch me. I can jump from here too." He launched himself from the side of the cliff, and she winced, praying he'd be fine. He landed with a loud splash, then propelled himself back toward her. "Come in. The water is fine. 'Tis just a wee bit cool. Ye get used to it quick because 'tis summer."

"I couldn't. I do not know how to swim. I am afraid of the water. Why, if I jumped, I'd surely never come up." She had a fear of the water but was embarrassed to admit it. She'd never had the opportunity.

"I'll help ye. See, just sit there on the side, pull off yer boots and hose, then put yer feet in the water. Ye'll see how quickly ye will adjust. And ye can kick. Practice kicking. 'Tis what will get ye back to the surface. Kicking."

Bess said, "I'm going to put my feet in. It looks quite refreshing and I have not done this since I was young."

Tryana watched Bess remove her boots and shoes, then moved over to a large flat rock at the edge and sat down, gingerly putting her toes in the water first. She gave a quick squeal, yanking her feet back out. "It's cold, Magni."

"Nay, 'tis no'. 'Tis most lovely." He jumped in from the side, then gave them a light splash. "Get yer feet wet, Ladylana. Ye'll feel better for it. Ye need no' get undressed. Just roll up yer trews."

She'd donned the trews Bess brought for her last eve just to keep her legs warm overnight. While it was entirely out of character for her, she removed her boots and hose, then rolled up her pant legs. Wiggling across the rock on her bottom until she reached the edge of the water, she did just what Bess had done with her toes and squealed even louder. "Cold!"

But then she put her feet in all the way, a smile crossing her face unlike she'd had in a long time. The cool water sluiced over her toes in a rush from the waterfall, and she couldn't stop herself from kicking, just as Magni had suggested.

As Tryana sat on the rock with her feet in the water, she couldn't help but feel a sense of relief. It had been months since she had enjoyed herself so, giggles erupting without even thinking about it. The cool water was exactly what she needed to wash away the stress of the last few months. The sensation of the water rushing over her toes and her legs was invigorating. She smiled, feeling grateful for Magni's suggestion. "Magni, this is still cold. How can you stand it?"

"I'm a warrior like my da. We dinnae get cold," he declared before jumping in again. His head bobbed out of the water and he whipped his hair sideways, sending water their way. "Besides, ye get used to it. After a while, ye canno' feel the cold at all."

As she sat with her legs dangling in the stream, Tryana couldn't help but feel a sense of longing. She wanted more than just these fleeting moments of peace and happiness. She wanted to spend the rest of her life with people like Cadyn and Magni and Bess. With her brother and his new wife Reyna. She wanted to experience everything Clan Ramsay had to offer, to learn to ride a horse well, feel the sun on her skin and the wind in her hair. She wanted to be free to learn how to swim and to make friends. A cool breeze brought her back to the reality of their situation.

"Magni, we should get out soon in case the men return." She hated to put an end to their fun, but they needed to move on. Find the abbey or Cadyn or Wulf. Someone to help her.

"I'm coming, Ladylana. Now I'm hungry." He headed toward her so she stood, drying herself off and lowering her pantlegs.

She noticed his shiver so moved over to his clothing, grabbing the tunic before she said, "Here, put this on. You're shivering."

He ran at her with such a force it surprised her. "Dinnae touch my things. I have something verra valuable in there." Launching himself with all his force, his slippery feet caused him to tumble and he barreled into her, his fist catching her in the eye.

"Careful, lad," Bess shouted. "Do not hurt my lady. Oh!"

Tryana let out a small cry, and her hand went straight to her eye. Tears welled in her eyes though she tried her best to hide them, but the sting was too much.

"Forgive me, Ladylana. I didnae mean to hurt ye. Please dinnae be mad at me. How bad are ye?"

"I'll be fine, Magni. I'm sure I already have a bruise from where the baron struck a couple of days ago."

Bess looked at her more closely and said, "Aye, you do have a bit of a bruise on your cheek. He hit you two or three times, if I recall."

"He's mean. If I see him, I'll punch him for

ye, Ladylana. Honorable Highlanders dinnae hit ladies."

So now she knew he had grown up somewhere in the Highlands. Lochluin Abbey was on the edge of the Highlands, so he could have met many Highlanders there, if that was where he lived. She decided not to pry anymore. It would wait. "Perhaps you should get dressed, Magni. I worry we'll be seen out here." She shook her head and found a dry rock to sit on, drying her feet and donning her hose and boots while she kept an eye on Magni. What was he hiding?

The lad dressed in a hurry then came over and set his elbows in her lap. "Ye arenae crying, are ye? Thor would never hit a lady. I didnae mean to so, please dinnae tell on me."

She squared her shoulders and said, "Magni, there is no one to tell so please do not worry yourself. I wish to hear if you've seen anyone or not. Did you check the area at all? You said you knew how to track. Did the men leave? Do you know which way they went?"

"Aye," he said, standing back so he could point. "They went that way. I saw the horse tracks, and they were no' fresh. They left last eve and have no' returned. Ye are safe with me, Ladylana."

"Many thanks to you, lad. Which is closer—Ramsay land or Lochluin Abbey?"

"Lochluin Abbey is that way." He pointed in the opposite direction from where the men went.

"Will you please take us there soon, lad?"

"I will, but I'll no' be staying. I like it here better."

She had so many unanswered questions about the lad that she wished to sit him down and answer them all, but she needed him, even though he was young. It wouldn't serve her purpose at all to anger the helpful lad.

"How many summers are you again, Magni?"

He shrugged his shoulders. "Eight." He picked up his things, made sure everything was there after turning his back to the two women.

If she had to, she'd guess the following:

Magni lived not far from here, possibly near Lochluin Abbey.

His name wasn't Magni.

His father wasn't Thor.

And he had something invaluable to him in his possession.

She'd have to uncover exactly what that was because she was getting an odd feeling in her belly.

CHAPTER TWELVE

THE GROUP LEFT at first light. They parted ways when they reached the main path off Ramsay land, Wulf and Reyna's group heading to York while Cadyn's group headed north toward the Highlands.

Once the group headed north, they traveled most of the day and didn't run into anyone who could give them any news. Tevis said, "I think we should stop on Cameron land. 'Tis less than two hours from here. We can sleep inside and eat good food. I have no' seen my grandparents in a while. And they receive news from the abbey. Lochluin Abbey receives so many visitors that they tend to hear things ahead of any others. They would know of any English garrisons passing through."

Tevis Massie's parents were Torcall Massie and Riley Cameron of Clan Cameron, though they lived on Black Isle with Clan Matheson because Torcall was a guard there. Riley's mother was Jennie Grant Cameron, a healer like Reyna and Isla's mothers were. And she was sister to his Aunt Brenna.

Dyna looked at Maitland who nodded his agreement. "It'll be our last warm meal, I will wager," Maitland said, looking at the sky for timing. "And the Cameron guards should have heard something. Ye know they learn much through the ones who travel to the abbey. If there is a garrison around, Brin will know it."

Brin was heir to the clan chief, Aedan Cameron, his only son.

"I wish yer mother would be here, Tevis. Is she no' a seer too?" Cadyn asked.

"Aye, but she does no' know Tryana, so she probably could no' help ye." He glanced at Dyna for confirmation of his statement and she nodded.

"'Tis verra rare for me to dream of someone I know little of. I have to be near them for a while." Dyna shrugged her shoulders. "I tell ye all that I see."

They arrived on Cameron land just around the supper hour. Brin greeted them with ten guards behind him. "I see Ramsay, Grant, and Menzie plaids so I know this group to be friendly. Welcome to Clan Cameron. Maitland, is that ye with Dyna Corbett? And is that my nephew Tevis with ye? I hope so."

"Aye, Brin. We seek a night's stay along with some warm food if ye have enough for our group."

"Ye are all welcome but since many of ye are cousins or closely related to my mother's family, please introduce yer group, Maitland."

"Tell me who ye know and then I'll go from there. Ye know Dyna and Tevis. Anyone else?"

"I know Dobbin and Cadyn, but I'm not familiar with the two in the back."

"Cadyn's sister Ceit is the golden-haired lass and Alaric is Jamie Grant's son."

Brin greeted them and said, "Welcome all. Join us for dinner. Dobbin, go on ahead and let my mother know ye are all here for supper. She'll be pleased, especially because Tevis is with ye."

Cadyn had been on Cameron land many times, but never in such a position. He wished to yell at the man and ask him what he knew of the English, but Dyna sent a look his way to let him know he needed to wait.

Dyna said, "Many thanks for yer hospitality, Brin. Before we move on and ye send yer guards back, may I ask if ye've received word of any English garrisons in the area?"

Brin replied, "Aye, we have. But we've no' met up with them. We heard they were nasty and roaming, yet we have no' been able to ascertain a purpose. We've no' searched on our own so I wager 'tis time to start. Know ye why they are in Scotland?"

"We'll explain over supper," Maitland said. "But if ye dinnae mind, we'd appreciate it if ye can send a couple of patrols out before dark with instructions to update us if they see any. Our king has asked us to follow them because we dinnae know their purpose. He fears castle sieges this far into Scotland."

"Aye." Brin spoke to one of his guards who gave the orders to the others and took their leave. "They'll apprise us of anything they uncover.

I gave them instructions not to engage, but to defend only. We are obligated, as ye know, to protect the abbey at all times so I appreciate the update."

They headed toward Cameron Castle, moving their horses inside the castle wall and to the stables. Maitland said, "We can take care of our horses after supper if ye dinnae have lodgings for them."

"Nay, we have plenty of stable lads and room for all."

Once there, they dismounted, the usual chatter sounded among the group. Cadyn said to his sister, "Ye are hale? Ye look ill or upset."

"Nay, I'm fine, Cadyn. Ye need no' watch over me. I can dismount on my own."

Cadyn shrugged and said, "As ye wish." Once he passed her, he noticed her foot caught on a strap and she nearly fell from her horse, but Brin managed to catch her.

Ceit grabbed onto Brin's shoulders before she tumbled arse over her feet. Brin set her to rights and said, "Ceit, if I recall correctly. Be careful."

Ceit blushed a shade Cadyn had never seen before, but Brin's tongue was tied. The two stared at each other much longer than usual. Then Cadyn smiled because he had the odd inkling that Ceit was smitten.

And so was Brin.

Ceit finally said, "My thanks to ye. My foot caught. Forgive me."

"Of course. Glad to help. Please come in and warm yerself by the fire." Ceit stepped ahead of

Brin and walked toward the hall, but not before she gave Cadyn a scowl that reminded him of when she was ten.

He let it pass, because he had more important things to think about.

Once inside, he greeted Jennie and Aedan Cameron, then settled at the table where Brin sat with Maitland and Dyna, the others in their group seated at a nearby trestle table. Tevis ran to visit with his grandparents at the dais along with Aedan's brother Ruari and his wife.

Now they could discuss this. Cadyn waited patiently while Maitland explained the issue with the baron and Tryana.

Brin asked, "Tryana's sire is who?"

"Wrath de Gray," Dyna replied. "Are ye familiar with him?"

Brin gave a low whistle. "Just that he is a mean bastard. His family lived not far from Lochluin Abbey long ago until his wife died. Then they moved to the Lowlands. But he was known for being a liar and a cheat. A gambler and a drinker."

Maitland declared, "And his son Wulf saw him push their mother down the staircase after she gave birth to her third child, a stillborn. Wrath claimed she fell and Wulf was just a lad so Wrath was never accused of anything. Wulf is searching for his sister in York. If she is no' there, they will be heading toward us."

Brin said, "So you are worried about the baron, not de Gray?"

Cadyn spoke up. "The baron is her betrothed and was cruel to Tryana when she first arrived at his home. I hate to see how he would treat her after they were married. She canno' marry him. No matter what de Gray says. She does no' want this marriage but her sire has already accepted coin for her and insists the marriage come to fruition."

Brin chuckled. "My guess would be that Wrath owed coin to the baron. He could have fostered his gambling debt to get the wife he wanted. I've heard of that happening before. The twisted have odd ways to control others and get what they want. The question is how to get Wulf's sister away from him."

"'Tis exactly the problem," Cadyn replied. "I think yer explanation makes perfect sense."

"How many in the baron's forces?"

"Less than two score," Cadyn said.

"And de Gray's?"

"That we dinnae know," Cadyn said, looking from Dyna to Maitland. "Have ye any idea?"

"Nay, but as I said before, the man is a gambler, so if he gambled well, he could have quite a bit of coin to hire men. Dinnae be surprised if he hires five score. I do believe he owns a castle in the Highlands."

"I doubt he gambled well. I like Brin's explanation," added Dyna. "If he has any men, it will probably be because the baron has hired them to see his wedding day come to fruition."

Maitland looked to Dyna and Cadyn. "We never heard of any other land he owned. I dinnae think Wulf is aware of this."

Cadyn stared at Dyna and then asked Brin, "Does it have towers? Is it near a waterfall?"

Brin shrugged his shoulder. "Ye know as well as I do that there are waterfalls all through the Lowlands and the Highlands. As for the towers? Aye, I think I heard it has two towers."

Just like in Cadyn's dream.

Reyna prayed they would find her husband's sister before too long. The poor lass had been through so much, she wondered how Tryana could keep a sound mind after all she'd been through. Seeing all their troubles made her appreciate how blessed her life had been on Black Isle. Plus the added blessing of so many clans they considered allies. She loved all her cousins dearly.

Did Wulf have any cousins at all? She had more than she could count.

Wulf slowed his horse as soon as they entered a small town in the Borderlands. There was a small group of soldiers standing in front of an inn, laughing and jesting with each other. "Those two men look familiar." He stopped to stare, watching them for a moment. "We'll stop to water the horses." He led them to a trough of water on the side of the road, climbing down before helping Reyna to dismount, but told Torrian's guards to patrol the town and return in half the hour.

Reyna patted her horse while she fed him an apple, then looked at Isla and said, "I'm starting to agree with Dyna and Cadyn. I feel like we are going in the wrong direction."

Isla glanced around at the area they were in. "Mayhap Wulf is about to discover a clue to her whereabouts. I dinnae know if we'll find anyone who can tell us anything for certain. All we need to know is if she's in York. If no', we head north."

Wulf strode straight over to Reyna and wrapped his arms around her, burying his face in her hair and whispering, "The one man I've seen with my sire. And the other one was with the baron. They will know." He lifted his head and scanned the area, apparently looking for anyone else he knew.

"They will not volunteer anything, Wulf. Ye must eavesdrop. Move closer."

"Aye, I wish to listen to their ramblings, see if we can learn anything at all." He stepped closer, moving his horse to the end of the trough while they settled the other horses.

"Sure is nice to be free of those two bastards for a while. We'll take our time arriving in the Highlands," a red-haired guard said.

The one who Wulf had seen with his sire was mostly bald. He said, "I'll not take too long as I have no idea how to travel there. It could take us forever if we get lost, and I'm not fond of gaining any more scars on my back from the evil bastard."

"We'll catch up with them easy enough. We just need to be there in a few more days."

Wulf listened a bit more but gained nothing. He sauntered back toward Reyna, Isla, and Grif.

Reyna whispered, "Did ye find out where the baron is? Where he went?"

"Nay. They discuss following someone but no

one mentions where they are headed. And no names."

Reyna said, "If ye two go inside the inn for a wee bit, leave us with the horses and we'll find out."

Wulf said, "I dinnae think I am fond of that idea." He crossed his arms and narrowed his gaze at his wife. "Exactly how do ye expect to find out?"

Grif ran his hand up and down Isla's back. "I think the lasses can cipher information from a group of men better than we can. We could step inside the inn and watch from there. Or enter the stable across the street." He pointed and Wulf glanced around him.

Reyna said, "He's right, husband." She knew they hadn't officially married yet, but they'd handfasted. That made it seem as though they were married, officially in a Scot's mind, and she loved using the word husband. Perhaps it was better if she didn't use his true name. She noticed Isla often did the same since they'd also handfasted. One never knew who was listening.

Grif wrapped his arm around Isla and tugged her close. "They are both far craftier than I am. And we'll no' be far."

Lewis said, "We'll watch from the other side of the area. Our arrows can hit faster than you can run."

Reyna looked at Isla and said, "I think we could come up with something. Five men, ye say. I think we can convince them to tell us where the baron is."

Wulf looked at Reyna, his eyes narrowed. "While I love the suggestion, I'm no' sure ye two are going to come up with the best idea nor do I like the idea of five men with two women. We may have to rescue ye."

Ysenda said, "There are seven of us plus the guards when they return. We can handle this, Wulf."

He let out a huge sigh and said, "I need to find Tryana. I'll trust ye." He kissed Reyna's cheek and said, "But dinnae give too much away to the men. I'll be watching."

Reyna shrugged and grinned.

Isla said, "If ye are that unsettled, then go in the stable. Thea and Ysenda can find a clear shot from across the way with their bow. The stable is right there. If anything untoward happens, ye can rescue us. Now go." She waved her hand at Wulf as if to send him off with such a small move.

Grif dropped his hand from Isla's shoulder and said, "Follow me, Wulf. Do it before the men go inside."

Reyna crossed her arms. "What can it hurt, Wulf? Give us a chance. A quarter hour is all we'll need."

Isla smirked and pushed her husband toward the stables. "Go and let us try."

Wulf said, "Say no more. I'm desperate so I'll allow this ridiculous idea. Promise to scream if ye need help. If ye are no' back signaling to us within a quarter hour, we're coming back." He and Grif headed toward the stable while the other three headed in the opposite direction.

Isla grinned at her. "We can do this." The two mounted their horses and took them away from the area so they could come in from the other side, giving the look of just arriving.

"Wait." Reyna smiled, then stopped to tug on her hair, yanking her plait out. She swung her hair free, the long dark waves falling down her back. "Now I'm ready. Follow me, Isla."

The two moved their horses off in a distance, then maneuvered them closer to the men. Three men greeted them, "Well, what have we here? Two beauties visiting us?"

Reyna fanned herself and scanned the area. "I do believe we are lost, Jennet."

Isla snorted, probably from the use of her mother's name. "Aye, Brigid," she said with emphasis. "I dinnae know this area."

Their mothers had been the best of friends just as she and Isla had been.

"It seems you are in the right place. Who are you looking for?" One of the guards drew closer, looking her up and down with a smile. "Your new love? Because you found me. I'm right here." His arms opened as if to take her in for a tight hug.

Reyna giggled and dismounted, nearly falling but the close guard caught her. Still laughing she righted herself and stared up into his brown eyes. "Do ye know where my uncle might live? I thought he lived in the Borderlands but we canno' find him. His name is Gareth Ward."

"Gareth Ward is your uncle?"

"Aye. We came for a visit. My sire will be along in about an hour."

The three men shared glances, then smiled, "Well, we can surely entertain you before your sire arrives, my lady. Would your sister like to join us?"

"Aye, but only for a short time."

"But we'd like to get to know you." The red-headed man was definitely the boldest.

"So where is my uncle Gareth's castle? Not far?" Reyna asked.

"You have a distance to go because he lives in York. But he's not there and won't be for a long time. He's in the Highlands so he'll not return for at least a fortnight." Baldie offered this information.

"The Highlands? But 'tis where we came from. We dinnae see him along the way."

One of the guards chuckled. "He does not want anyone to see him. There is a hidden path to this castle. Belongs to a friend of his. North of Perth. He'll be gone for a long time."

"Aye, not far from Dulnain Valley, I believe. We've got all the time in the world to have some fun."

Isla said, "I've heard enough. Let's take our leave, cousin."

One guard scowled and grabbed Reyna's arm, pulling her back against him. "She's staying. You can leave."

Reyna laughed and leaned back close to him, then brought her booted heel up behind her just so to catch the man in his bollocks. He fell forward with a groan, but one of the others reached for her.

Wulf's voice carried through the silence like a blade meant to kill. "Unhand my wife!"

A shadow flew through the area and the other two men were on the ground before Reyna could tell him she had everything under control. Wulf beat one down while the second jumped on his back, but he deftly flipped the man head over arse, flat onto his back hard enough to knock the wind out of him.

He stood up and brushed the dirt from his hands before holding one out to his wife. "My lady. Ye did a fine job." And he gave her a full bow.

Reyna experienced a hot flash unlike she'd ever faced, her voice coming out in a husky undertone that raised her husband's one eyebrow. "Oh, husband. Ye are so fine when ye fight for me."

He whispered in her ear, "Ye'll find out how fine my love is for ye later. Hellfire, but ye are one amazing woman, my lady."

Reyna gave him a saucy look after he lifted her up onto her horse.

"Off to the Highlands we go," Wulf said. "I think I know exactly where we are going."

"Where?" Grif asked.

"A dilapidated castle my sire claimed a long time ago. I thought he sold it, but mayhap no'."

Reyna said, "I hope we meet up with Maitland and the others."

"We probably will."

"Why are ye so sure?" Wulf asked.

Isla said, "Even I can answer that. Cadyn and Dyna were right. Sounds like they are at the same castle that Cadyn dreamed Tryana was at. And they are already there or on their way, I am sure of it."

"And this time, I'll put an arrow in my sire's black heart. I should have done it the first time when I had the chance." Wulf reached over and squeezed his wife's hand. "Ye are such a gift to me, Reyna Matheson."

CHAPTER THIRTEEN

TRYANA FINISHED HER ablutions while Magni made a meal of the dried meat that Bess had brought and the hunk of cheese they had. When she finished, she said, "I have a favor to ask, Magni. Will ye teach me how to use your bow, if you please?"

"Aye. We can try to get a rabbit for dinner."

"But Bess and I would like to go to Lochluin Abbey. If we can get there, someone would help us fight off the mean baron who is chasing us. And I'm sure they would feed all of us."

"Aye, I can show ye how to use my bow now, if ye like. Then we can head to the abbey after high sun."

"How long will it take us to get there?" She wondered if she could trust everything the lad told her, but she had no alternative.

"Probably three hours. If we had horses, less than an hour. And Cameron land is right there. Do ye know any of the Camerons? They are verra nice."

"Nay, I do not know anyone there."

Pieces of the puzzle were starting to fall into place about this mysterious lad and his journey.

He finished his meal and said, "Come, we can go now."

It turned out that Magni was a very good teacher. He showed her how to hold the bow, how to turn her body, and how to aim. Surprised at his talent, she listened to everything he told her, and he did manage to kill one rabbit for dinner. They all cheered when they noticed the rabbit fall in the small knoll in front of them.

Cheering was a big mistake.

Almost instantly, about a score of horses came out of the surrounding forest at the same time. Tryana and Bess ran, headed back toward the waterfall, but Magni climbed a tree.

Something she should have done.

Tryana ran in a different direction from Bess, successfully drawing at least a dozen men to follow her and pulling them away from Magni and Bess. Two tried to reach down and scoop her up but she fought, biting one man's arm who then let go, and using a branch she'd picked from the ground to strike another man in the face. Glad that she'd put on the trews, she had the ability to run between trees and brush where the horses couldn't follow.

She ran and ran for what seemed like an hour, though she was nowhere near the waterfall anymore. Her gaze was on the lookout for any hiding place, but nothing materialized. The men yelled at each other constantly, but she ignored them, knowing that if she heard the baron's voice or her father's, she'd become overwhelmed with fear.

Better to think of them as a group of reivers after an innocent woman.

She broke through the forest into a meadow, the grassland not too deep so she could run faster.

"Get her!" That voice belonged to the baron, and that was not what she needed. She stumbled, her boot catching in a hole in the ground, but she regained her balance quickly.

But just as she thought she had a clear path, something caught her foot. Tryana stumbled and fell, tumbling head over heels in the grass. She looked up to see a man had hopped off his horse and grabbed her ankle, his face twisted in an angry snarl.

Without hesitation, Tryana kicked out with her other foot, connecting with the man's jaw. He let go, groaning in pain, and she scrambled to her feet, ready to run again. But more men had appeared, surrounding her on all sides. Their faces were cruel, their eyes glinting with malice.

Tryana knew she was outnumbered and outmatched. She had no weapon, no way to defend herself. For the first time, she had to accept that this could be worse than she thought. What if they didn't care if she lived? She thought the baron still wanted her for his bride, but perhaps he was tiring of the fight. It was entirely possible that she was going to die here, alone in a field with no one to mourn her passing.

One small satisfaction came to her. They hadn't

gotten Bess or Magni. Well, she'd go along with them if they spared her two friends.

But as the men closed in, Tryana felt a surge of anger. She would not let them take her without a fight. She balled her hands into fists and stood her ground. She tried to fight, glad to see it wasn't the baron who'd caught her, but this guard was huge. She bit him and he cursed, so he held her down and tied her hands. Then he held her in a mighty grip and waited for the baron to approach them.

He looked at her with disgust. "You think to marry me in trews? You will learn to act respectably. Running away and wearing men's clothing is far from respectable. You'll be feeling my whip soon enough."

The man she rode with chuckled and said, "Cannot wait to see this bitch get her just due. Why not right here, Baron?"

"She will be punished soon enough. First she'll say her prayers and then she'll receive her penance. I do prefer to have women tended by a healer after their whipping. Seems the right thing to do and we are on the road, so this will wait. Do not forget that we are in Scotland and not in England. No one will give me the respect I deserve. Soon enough, but first we head north."

North? Where the hell was the man taking her?

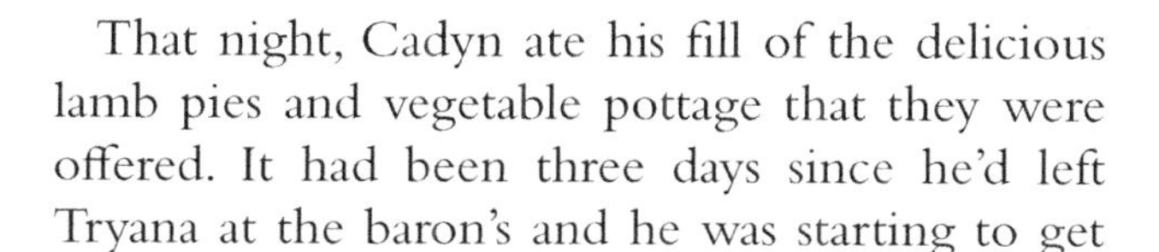

That night, Cadyn ate his fill of the delicious lamb pies and vegetable pottage that they were offered. It had been three days since he'd left Tryana at the baron's and he was starting to get unsettled about finding her. He pushed back from the table, wishing to go out to patrol on his own when the door opened and three of the Cameron guards entered.

Brin waved them over, and his father joined him. "What did ye find?"

"Believe it or no', we found several odd Englishmen on horseback. Not traveling together as a garrison but as if they were searching for something. We each caught different men on the hunt, though they were no' using their bows. We followed for a wee bit and discovered naught, so I gathered five of our men and we stopped to question two of them, asking them why they were on Cameron land.

"They claimed ignorance, said they lost a hunting dog and were searching for it, but we dinnae believe them. It was as though one man was creating the story while the others went along."

"What area of our land?" Aedan asked. "Because ye are to send them off, as ye know."

"We escorted them off our land, but my wager is they will return shortly. They were on the south edge. We also saw a few near the waterfall farther south, and they also were searching for something."

"As long as they are off our property," Aedan said.

Brin said, "I dinnae like it. Something is up. Send the men out again. I think ye'll find them in the same spot. Whatever they are doin', 'tis no' good. 'Tis nearly dark so they'll be up to something. I'll join ye."

His father said, "Dinnae go far. Mayhap they are looking to overtake the abbey."

Maitland said, "I'll go with ye."

Cadyn was already standing, ready to go, as were Dyna, Tevis, Ceit, and Alaric, but Brin said, "The three of us will go. Ye remain here in case anything else happens. We shall return post haste."

Maitland added, "We'll only go to the waterfall and return, see if they are still there."

The door flew open and a dark-haired lad not yet ten flew across the hall, tears covering his face. "Brin, ye must help me. Please. Those mean men, they..." He stopped in front of Brin and tugged on his tunic as he paused to catch his breath. The lad was exhausted and had clearly been running for some time.

"Sit, Perrin. What happened?"

"I canno' sit. Ye have to save her. She was verra nice and I was teaching her how to shoot a bow and the men came out of everywhere, stealing her away."

Brin looked at Maitland. "I think we have our explanation as to what the English were lookin' for. Perrin, where were ye, and how long did it take ye to get here?"

Cadyn had this odd chill come up his spine at the same time that Dyna turned to look at him. "Could it be?"

"Ye think 'tis the lass ye are seeking?" Brin asked.

"She's a long way from York," Maitland argued.

"But Dyna and I both dreamed she was in the Highlands. It could be her." Cadyn crossed his arms, confident that this could be the clue they were looking for, even if she'd been captured an hour away. "She could have escaped and then caught again."

"Aye!" Perrin said. "She said she ran away from these evil men. They followed us into the cave behind the waterfall, but they could no' find my secret wall." The lad looked as smug as anyone he'd ever seen, proud of his hidden wall.

"So ye all stayed behind the waterfall?" Dyna asked. "When did ye first see her?"

"Last eve I saved her and her maid. So we slept there, then I was jumping over the falls for my bath and she yelled at me to be careful. Then she wanted me to show her how to shoot my bow so I did and we got one rabbit and we all cheered but then the men came out of the woods. At least a score, Brin. She ran and ran and they got her in the meadow and tied her up. And her maid was with her. Bess was her name. But she said she was going to run away and go home. She went the opposite way."

"All right. We'll go take a look right now, Perrin. Ye can ride with me, but if we are outnumbered, we'll come back for more guards," Brin said. "We have to move swiftly if we are to catch them before they move on."

Brin, Perrin, Cadyn, and Maitland rode out to the south edge of the Cameron land, keeping a sharp eye out for any signs of the Englishmen. "Is this the right area, Perri?" Brin slipped back into calling him the pet name for the lad when he was younger.

"Aye. We were at the waterfall and she ran toward the meadow. I ran the other way and so did Bess, her friend."

As they approached the waterfall, they heard a rustling in the bushes. Maitland signaled to Brin to dismount, and they stealthily made their way towards the sound.

As they got closer, they could see two Englishmen huddled together, speaking in hushed tones. They couldn't make out what they were saying but they could tell it was urgent. Suddenly, one of the men pulled out a map and began pointing to different spots on it, all the while looking around to make sure they weren't being watched.

Brin, Cadyn, and Maitland exchanged a quick glance, both realizing that this was definitely no hunting excursion. Cadyn came out of the bushes, his sword in front of him. "Where is she?"

The two men jumped to their feet, shocked to be found, the two glancing over Cadyn's shoulder to see who else was behind him. "Who? Where is who?"

"A young lass. Brown hair. Blue eyes. The one ye stole away earlier."

The one man stared at the other and then held his hands up in surrender. "We were with the baron's group until they kidnapped the woman. We stayed back because we do not wish to be part of this any longer."

"Why no'?" Maitland asked.

"Because the baron is taking her into the Highlands. I did not agree to go that far. I'm returning to England where it's safer. I prefer to stay in the Borderlands. It is safer there and much to steal, if you know what I mean."

"Ye are reivers? No' employed by the baron?" Cadyn asked with derision.

"Aye, they paid us good coin to get her there, then more to bring her back. We've seen enough of his cruelty. He uses his fists on the poor lass. I don't mind punching men, but not young lasses. He tied the one up and took her with him, then sent another group home with the maid. Said he would only handle one woman from here."

The fury built inside Cadyn so much that he didn't dare speak. Maitland clasped his shoulder and said to the men, "Then do the right thing and tell us exactly where they are taking her. If ye do we'll allow ye to go on yer way. If ye dinnae help us, we'll take ye to the magistrate or to Logan Ramsay who is on his way here."

The one man's eyes widened and he barked out, "I'll tell all. They are taking her to a castle north of Perth. A path near two opposing oaks. In Dulnain Valley. That's all we know."

The group left the men and headed back to Cameron Castle. "I'd feel better if we knew for certes it was Wulf's sister," Maitland said. "Mayhap the baron stole himself another lass as a plaything."

Cadyn looked over at the lad and said, "Perrin, can ye answer a question for me? Think really hard. Did she tell ye what her name was?"

Perrin thought for a moment, then his eyes widened and he smiled.

"Ladylana."

CHAPTER FOURTEEN

THEY UPDATED THE group back on Cameron land, then made plans to head into the Highlands. It was their only option, as far as Cadyn could see. There was no point in delaying either.

Cadyn mounted his horse ahead of everyone, Dyna and Brin directly behind him.

"Did ye wish to consider whether or not it is Tryana first?" Dyna yelled at him. "The name isn't right."

"Close enough for me," Cadyn yelled back. "Lads never get names correct, but ye would no' know that, Dyna. Ye have lasses."

Dyna glanced over at Brin who was nodding with a grin. "He's right. Though we do have one lad, I'll no' argue yer reasoning. Even Derric canno' repeat names to me. Where are ye going, Cadyn?"

"North. She's heading north into the Highlands as the reivers told us. I believe them because they had no reason to lie. 'Tis my sense of what is happening anyway. Dyna's dream of the waterfall was true, and mine concerns an old tower. I suspect 'tis the one owned by de Gray. The baron has her and he's taking her to de Gray's castle where there are two opposing oaks on the path, but I dinnae know exactly where."

"I'll follow. Go. Take the main path to see if ye can track them," Brin said. "Dyna can tell from riding at a top speed."

The only problem was that it was dark. Much more difficult to see anyone's tracks, but they'd be moving slower too. "I'm no' worried. They dinnae know the Highlands like we do."

"Verra true," Dyna said.

They split into two groups, Perrin riding with Brin. Maitland led the group that was to fan out and patrol deeper into the forests while Dyna, Cadyn, Alaric, and Brin were charging forward knowing the bastard had at least an hour on horseback ahead of them. Alaric, being a Grant, would know the area better.

About half into the hour, Cadyn noticed something unusual. He slowed his horse when he caught something out of the corner of his eye, a path that had recently been taken based on the broken bushes. Either that or a herd of deer had just run through.

"I see it, Cadyn," Dyna said. "We need to follow it. This was done by multiple large animals."

They took the path at a slower pace because it wasn't the main path, and it was deep in the forest. Dyna rode ahead of Cadyn because she was the better tracker. Every time she slowed, she pointed in a different direction and they followed. Cadyn was amazed at her instinct.

Within a quarter hour, sounds of a group settling for the night could be heard. They were rather raucous, but soon enough, they discovered why. As soon as Dyna set eyes on the group, she spun around on her horse and said, "Ramsay, ye'll not move until we make a plan. We are heavily outnumbered. Nearly a score to four."

"Five," Perrin whispered. "I have my bow."

"Is this the group, Perri?" Brin asked, moving abreast of Cadyn so they could observe the group from a well-hidden spot in the trees.

"Aye. 'Tis Ladylana they are tying to the tree. We have to save her. Look, he has a whip." Perrin pointed, then covered his mouth with this hand.

"Cadyn…"

"'Tis Tryana, for certes." Cadyn had to contain his emotions, rein them in because he knew Dyna was right. They had to have a plan.

Dyna whispered, "I count six and ten against our five." Then she smiled, nodding behind them. "Seems we have three more. Now those are better numbers." Maitland, Ceit, and Tevis appeared behind them.

Tevis said, "We'll help. Our numbers are good against the English."

Dyna said, "Perfect. Dobbin, slinger. Ceit, Cadyn, Perrin, and I will use bows. Brin, Maitland, Alaric, and Tevis, use your swords around the periphery. We'll go after the men in the center. Aim to wound unless they attack us. They are English. We must have good reason to kill them."

"He's going to whip her. Look!" Perrin pointed to the middle of the scene where the baron stood behind Tryana who was bound to a tree, her back to the baron as he flicked his wrist with a cracking whip.

"Nay, he's no'," Cadyn declared, taking his bow and aiming carefully.

Dyna said, "His shoulder, Cadyn. Now. Go. Everyone."

Other arrows sluiced through the trees at the same time Cadyn's caught the baron's shoulder, forcing him to drop the whip. He spun around and pulled out his small sword, running straight for them. But once he saw the number of Highlander guards coming at him, he turned around and ran the other way.

Cadyn had eyes only for Tryana. He used his bow to wound two others who went down immediately, but the rest crumpled to the ground quickly after their short assault. Most of the baron's men had no interest in fighting, three men surrendering without a fight.

He headed for Tryana.

As he approached the tree where Tryana was bound, Cadyn could see the fear in her eyes. Her wrists were rubbed raw from the rough rope that held her in place, and her tunic was torn in several places from the struggle.

He was going to kill the Baron of Topcliffe.

Tryana closed her eyes because she didn't wish to see the whip before it struck her. She knew from experience that for her, it was better for whatever punishment she was to receive to be a surprise.

So she closed her eyes and waited for the sound of the whip but it never came. Instead the baron's squeal forced her eyes open as she turned her head around to see what had happened.

Stunned was the only thing she could say.

Sheer chaos reigned as arrows sluiced through the air, connecting with the baron's men. One was hit in the head with a stone, knocking him out.

And then another.

Who was here?

She strained, but her hands were bound on the other side of the tree which severely limited her chance to see what was happening.

Then she saw him.

Cadyn. Fighting his way toward her, looking like the finest warrior in all of the land. He had a bow out but then dropped it and retrieved his sword. The baron bled profusely and ran in the opposite direction.

Some of the baron's men held their hands up, dropping their weapons before they surrendered. It wasn't much of a battle as it didn't last long, but there was blood, and she had hope that this ridiculous betrothal would finally be ended.

When he was done battling the baron's men, Cadyn strode toward her, the look on his face triumphant, and she had the oddest feeling that this was the man she should be marrying.

"Cadyn, how did you find me?"

Cadyn kissed her forehead before he reached

around to cut her bindings. As soon as she was free, she threw her arms around his neck and let out a few tears, but she had so many questions.

He pulled back to look at her, his eyes searching her face for any signs of injury. While she had some bruises on her face along with her raw wrists, he felt a wave of relief wash over him that she stood in front of him.

He knew that the emotional scars would take longer to heal. Tryana had been through a traumatic experience, and it would take time for her to recover.

But he would be there for her. Whatever she needed.

"How did you know?" she whispered.

"Yer friend, Perrin, came to tell us. We were at Cameron Castle just finishing supper when he came in telling us we need to save ye from the mean men."

"Perrin?" Her gaze scanned the area, then she saw Magni, who had just come out of the trees and was running directly at her.

"Ladylana! We saved ye!" He gave her a big hug.

"You did. I cannot thank you enough, Magni."

"Hush," he whispered, holding his finger to her lips. "Dinnae call me that. They dinnae know who I truly am. 'Tis a big secret. I'll explain when we get back."

"All right." She glanced at Cadyn but he shrugged.

"Please. Promise me ye'll keep my secret until the morrow. Please?" He looked from Cadyn to Tryana and back again.

"I promise. You come to me on the morrow and we'll discuss it. This night is for celebrating." The name she heard Cadyn use gave her an odd inkling, but she would honor his request. She definitely needed to learn more about Perrin, or Magni, whichever name was correct.

"Aye," he said, the worry disappearing from his face as he jumped up and clapped hands. "We saved ye." Then he spun around and headed back into the group. "Brin, did ye see my arrow? Who did I hit?"

Cadyn asked, "What was that about?"

"I promised the lad. I'll tell you on the morrow. For this night, he is whomever he wishes to be."

By the time they returned to their horses, Maitland and the other guards joined them. He said, "Well done. I see ye have found one garrison. My group will take care of them if ye wish to head back. I plan to have a wee chat with the baron after I tie him up. Make him understand that he has no claim on ye, lass. I'll find a way to convince him."

"Many thanks to you."

"Ye look exhausted, Tryana. Take her back to Cameron Castle, Cadyn. Jennie will take good care of her. Her wrists are raw and her face is bruised."

Cadyn led her to his horse, putting his hands around her waist to lift her onto the saddle. The wee lass weighed nearly nothing after all she'd been through.

"Cadyn. My brother? Have ye seen Wulf? Is he here?" Her gaze searched the area but then came back to him. The hope in her eyes was something he wasn't used to seeing.

"Nay. He and Reyna went to York looking for ye. Dyna and I thought ye were in the Highlands so we came in this direction. He'll follow us eventually. Mayhap in a day or two he'll join us." He mounted behind her while Brin and Perrin joined them along with Dyna.

Brin said, "I'll head back with ye. Maitland will take care of the rest. He can decide who stays and who goes."

Once they were on the main path, they settled on a comfortable trot for the horses. Cadyn had to admit he quite liked having the lass in front of him. He'd finally been able to calm down from seeing the whip in the baron's hands. "Do ye know where he was taking ye, lass?"

Tryana said, "The only thing I ever overheard was that we were going deep into the Highlands to some crumbling castle that had one tower still usable. I don't know exactly where, but they were careful to stay off the main road."

"And why was he planning to whip ye?"

"Because I ran away. We met Perrin and hid behind the waterfall, but they caught us the next day. That and he said I had penance for wearing a man's trews."

"I think ye wear them nicely. In my clan, ye see lasses in trews more than gowns. It makes sense, especially when riding a horse."

Tryana smiled at Cadyn's words and leaned back slightly into his chest. She couldn't help but feel safe with him, even though they had just met a short time ago. "I'm glad you think so. The baron and his men, however, do not share the same sentiment," she said with a small chuckle.

Cadyn couldn't help but chuckle with her. "Aye, they seem to be more focused on outdated traditions than practicality for a lass. But they are English. We Scots think on what's best."

They rode in comfortable silence for a while, enjoying the peace and quiet of the Highlands. Tryana wished she had more experience in the real world. Living with her aunt and uncle near the Borderlands had kept her from making friends, so she had no experience at all with lads.

"Cadyn, I know you said you were not betrothed, but do you have a special girlfriend at home? Someone you hope to marry someday?" She didn't know a better way to ask, so decided being honest was the best way to handle her questions.

Cadyn leaned forward and whispered into her ear, "Nay, I've never had my eye on anyone but ye."

His warm breath against her ear made her shiver, a small smile creeping across her face because his answer pleased her. "Look, we are nearly on Cameron land. I'll show ye my favorite spot once we are safely on their land."

She said, "I would like that. But how do ye know this land so well? Why have you traveled here so often?

"My aunt Brenna is sister to Jennie Cameron. They are both wonderful healers so I've been here many times. We come if we are ever on a journey, and we are in need of a healer, and we came many times just for the two to visit. Aunt Brenna and Jennie can chatter on for days."

"Two healers in the family? How fortunate ye are."

"We are. And their daughters both became healers, along with my cousin, but they all live on Black Isle with Clan Matheson."

"In other words, Cadyn MacAdam, you have friends everywhere."

He chuckled and replied, "Everywhere but England."

They traveled about another half an hour when the Cameron Castle came into view. Once they were close, Cadyn called out to Brin, "I'll meet ye back at the castle. I'm taking Tryana to the hill."

Brin nodded, then moved on.

She couldn't help but wonder what was so special about the hill. He took a path that led behind Lochluin Abbey. They passed a small hill with no trees on it. Cadyn said, "That hill 'tis Aedan's favorite. Mine is farther into the forest."

A bit later, he stopped his horse in front of a loch with a small hill next to it. "This is my favorite place. In fact, Jennie had a cottage made near here. This loch is so warm that I believe it has special springs underneath it, but the hill makes you feel like ye are close to the sky. He found a spot to leave his horse, attaching the reins to a nearby bush.

He lifted her down and took her hand in his, leading her over to the small hill. "Can ye manage in yer boots? 'Tis dark, but the moonlight is enough on the hill." Once they reached the top, he said, "Tell me what ye think. I feel as if I could reach up for one of the stars this eve."

She stood and tipped her head back, the multitude of stars now overhead. "Oh, Cadyn. 'Tis beautiful. I think I can touch the sky." She reached up, then giggled, casting a quick look his way.

His eyes were on her, his gaze darkened. He stilled and said, "May I kiss ye, Tryana?"

"Kiss me?" She tried to hide the panic in her voice. "It would please me, Cadyn, but you are the only man I've ever kissed. Please know that I am inexperienced. I know little of relationships between men and women."

Cadyn stepped closer to her, his hand cupping her cheek. "Ye need not worry, lass. I will guide ye." He leaned in, his lips brushing against hers as he whispered, "Ye taste sweet as the berries in the field."

Tryana's heart raced as he deepened the kiss, his tongue seeking entrance to her mouth. She let out a soft moan, her arms wrapping around his neck. He pulled her closer, his hands roaming down her back. She felt a warmth spread through her, a feeling she had never experienced before.

She broke the kiss, gasping for air. "Cadyn, I..."

"Do ye wish for me to stop, lass? Just say so and I will." He brushed the back of his fingers against her cheek. "Ye are so beautiful, Tryana."

How did she tell him that she wished this would never end? "Nay, please do not stop."

Cadyn leaned down and captured her lips in

a searing kiss, his hands roaming over her body. Tryana moaned, pressing herself closer to him, her hands fisting in his hair. Everything about this man pleased her, but she was more confused than anything. What was she supposed to do?

As the kiss deepened, Tryana felt her worries and uncertainties melt away. Cadyn's touch and the way he made her feel were all she could focus on. She parted her lips, inviting him in, and he eagerly accepted. The kiss became more passionate, more urgent, and Tryana felt a desire within her that she never knew existed.

But she also had an odd fear of what was to come, simply because she had no idea what took place between lovers.

As if sensing her hesitation, Cadyn pulled away from the kiss, his breaths coming out in ragged pants. He looked down at her with such a fierce intensity that it made her pulse quicken. "Ye are mine, Tryana. And I am yours," he said, his voice low and husky. "We need no' pretend to know everything about love and passion. We will learn together."

Tryana felt her heart swell with affection for him. She had never met anyone like him before. He was kind, gentle, and patient with her in a way that no one else had ever been. She knew that she wanted to be with him, to explore the depths of passion and love that they could share together.

He kissed a trail down her neck to the fine bone across her chest, her breath coming in short pants.

Just when she was about to ask him what to do next, he ended his exploration, cupping her face. "'Tis too soon for us to go further. Enough for this night. I seem to have forgotten yer wounds need tending. I'll take ye back to the castle. They will be expecting us soon."

He helped her back to their horse and lifted her onto his mount before climbing on behind her. Suddenly, she was very concerned. "Cadyn, I did not disappoint you, did I?" Her mind couldn't help but wonder what she could have done to make the experience better. What exactly was a lass to do?

"Never, lass. Ye will never disappoint me."

She turned around so he wouldn't see her wide smile.

CHAPTER FIFTEEN

WHEN TRYANA AWAKENED the next morn, she couldn't help but smile. This was the first time in a very long time that she hadn't awakened with a heavy heart.

Instead, her heart was bursting with happiness and the possibility of a better life thanks to Cadyn and all the others who had rescued her from the baron's clutches. But she still had a few things that needed to be taken care of, and she hoped to complete her tasks on this day. Jennie Cameron had rubbed a salve on her wrists that made the pain nearly go away. She would visit her again this morn to make sure they were healing properly. Then she had many things to see to.

First, she hoped that Wulf would be arriving today. True, Cadyn and Dyna had both thought it would be another day or two before they arrived, but she hoped it would be sooner. She had something important to do at Lochluin Abbey, and she wanted Wulf with her for her task. She needed to tell Wulf everything. No more secrets. It was time to reveal her sire for the monster he was.

Secondly, she had to speak with Magni to find out his true identity. Perhaps she could convince him to go with her to the abbey since he was familiar with it. She needed to speak with the nuns about what happened so many years ago.

She finished her ablutions and headed down the staircase, surprised that the hall was nearly empty. Dyna and Jennie Cameron were seated near the hearth, chatting. As soon as they saw her, Jennie came to her aid. "Please have a seat by the fire where it is warm. 'Tis a gray day outside and cool for late summer. I'll have the serving lass bring ye a bowl of oats and honey. And I'll bring the salve so we can tend yer wrists again before the day begins. Will that suit ye? There is fruit on the chest next to the hearth."

The chieftain's wife was as sweet as anyone she'd ever met. "That all sounds wonderful, and I am most grateful for your hospitality."

Jennie headed toward the kitchen so she sat in the chair closest to the hearth, anxious for a bit of warmth. "Good morn to ye, Dyna. My thanks again."

"Ye need not thank me anymore. 'Twas the right thing to do. We witnessed the baron's cruelty so he'll not get his hands on ye again, or I'll threaten him."

That vision made her smile. "Where is everyone?"

"Out hunting. Brin and Uncle Aedan love a bit of a challenge. With this many archers, Uncle Aedan is hoping for a big boar to roast or mayhap a deer. And Brin loves pheasant. With all these archers, he decided to take advantage of their skills. They gain boasting skills and food to roast."

Jennie came back into the hall with a goblet of warm broth for her, setting it on the table closest to her. "Yer oats will be here soon. I heard yer conversation. Aedan loves to hunt. He was never much of a warrior, was always more interested in the stars in the night sky, but he loves the challenge of hunting." She reached for Tryana's wrists and rubbed the salve wherever her tender skin was raw from the rope abrasions.

Once Jennie finished, she thanked her and took the goblet from her skilled hands. Tryana sipped the warm treat, sighing with pleasure as it warmed her insides. "What are yer plans, Dyna? Will ye wait for Wulf and Reyna?"

Dyna leaned back in her chair and stared at the overhead beams. "I didnae expect to be this close to home. If we were a bit closer, I might try a quick jaunt home to visit Derric and my bairns. But to answer yer question, Maitland and I have decided to await Wulf's arrival to see what he's uncovered first. Maitland's group saw no English garrison. We took care of one, and he has sent the group to the local sheriff to decide what to do with them, but I suspect the Ramsay guards may escort them back to England. We dinnae know the existence of the other garrison. 'Tis possible Wulf and Reyna may encounter them. We hope they'll return on the morrow, and Aunt Jennie and Uncle Aedan have graciously extended our welcome for a few days, whatever is necessary."

"Ye are always welcome, and ye know it. Since

our daughters live on Black Isle, we are often lonely and miss family. Is there anything ye would like to do, Tryana? I have heard yer life has been difficult, but I dinnae wish to pry. I'll help ye find some new clothes—gowns or trews—whatever ye prefer."

"That would be wonderful. This gown you found for me last eve is lovely, but I would appreciate a pair of trews for a lass, if you have any. Mayhap one more gown. I'd like to continue learning archery, so I could wear the trews while I practice. But do you think it would be possible for me to visit the abbey? We lived not far from here when we were young, and my mother attended chapel often. I would love to visit and see if any of the nuns remember me or my mother." If Wulf didn't arrive today she would have to go to the abbey without him. Her errand there couldn't wait any longer.

"Of course. I'll search for some of Gwyneth's fine leggings she used to make for my daughters."

"Leggings?" This was a term she was unfamiliar with.

"Gwyneth Ramsay's creation for lasses who wish to be active. They fit a bit tighter than trews and are verra stretchy. She goes to Edinburgh for the fabric."

"That sounds wonderful."

"And someone will take ye to the abbey. Aedan's brother Ruari watches over it and manages the guards there. He knows the nuns better than I do these days. He can introduce ye to the ones who have been there the longest. And ye are always welcome at the chapel, lass. 'Tis for everyone."

Dyna said, "Once ye finish breaking yer fast, I'll take ye there. I need to take my horse on a good gallop across the meadow." The serving lass brought a bowl of oats for her sweetened with honey along with a baked apple. It was as sweet as anything she'd had of late.

They made small talk while she finished her food, but as soon as she finished, Jennie stood up. "Let me search for some clothes while Dyna takes ye to the abbey."

As soon as she was finished, Jennie hurried in and said, "Here. I found a pair of Tara's leggings and a tunic. Ye are welcome to them. She has all she needs now that she lives in the same clan as Gwyneth's daughter Brigid. I think these will fit ye."

"Many thanks to ye," she said, taking the leggings and trying them on in the healing chamber. She stepped out and said, "My, but these are quite fine and comfortable. Are you ready, Dyna?"

The two headed toward Lochluin Abbey, enjoying the beautiful day. Many fluffy clouds kept the sun from being out for too long but it was warm and dry. She'd hoped to see the hunters but since they crossed a meadow to get to the abbey, she wasn't surprised to see it empty. Hunting was much better in the forests.

They rode quietly, Tryana pleased that the horse Dyna found for her was a calm mare. She didn't have much experience riding, but enough.

This proved to be a wonderful day for practice. A sense of calm overwhelmed her, the fear of the baron gone, the wonder of what life would bring her now overpowering the thoughts of not being good enough, of the fear of marriage, of a cruel man in her life every day.

The only part that was missing at the moment was her dear brother. How she wished he would be with her when she approached the nuns about the past. While he had no knowledge of what transpired years ago, his presence would be comforting. She loved her brother fiercely because he was her only sibling.

Or was he?

The peace and quiet were refreshing, and she took a deep breath of the fresh air, tipping her face back to the cool breeze.

As they approached the abbey, they could hear the faint sound of music coming from inside. It was a beautiful melody, slow and melancholic, but with a hint of hope woven into the notes. They followed the sound until they reached the stables for the abbey.

She stopped her horse near the entryway, listening to the music and watching the monks as they played their instruments. It was a peaceful moment, and she felt grateful for being able to witness it.

Two stable lads greeted them and took the horses in for a brushing. Dyna said, "Shall I go in with ye? I dinnae know the nuns, but I think the eldest one is Sister Matilda, if I recall."

"I can manage on my own. Many thanks,"

Tryana said as she walked toward the front entryway.

Dyna called out, "I'll be in the stables chatting with Ruari. I'm sure he's here because I can hear his voice down at the end."

Tryana waved to acknowledge that she heard her, then marched over to the door, one foot in front of the other. The music had stopped, the sound coming from open windows in the middle of the abbey. The monks were probably on to their next task, just as she was. Coming back to Lochluin Abbey was something she'd planned to do for years. She would not stop until she found out the truth. Her hands visibly shook as she approached the door. How she prayed that she would receive good news about the result of all that had transpired so long ago.

Once inside, a young nun greeted her, bowing briefly. She folded her hands in front of her and said, "Greetings to you, Sister. I am staying with the Camerons and my name is Tryana de Gray. Would Sister Matilda be available?" She heard the slight tremor in her voice, but hoped the nun hadn't noticed.

"Aye, I'll find her for you. Have a seat in the small library over there, if you please."

Tryana stepped inside the chamber full of books, impressed by how large the bookcase was, covering one entire wall. She ran her fingers across the bindings, recalling how her mother would borrow books occasionally to teach her how to read. Her other fond memory was finding a wonderful book to curl up with on the floor while her mother went about her business. Time flitted away whenever she could step into a different world with new characters who soon became her friends.

Her mind traveled back to that fateful day eight years ago when she'd been given a task to complete and told to keep her task a secret. She was not allowed to tell anyone where she'd gone or why. At the tender age of ten winters, she'd always done what she'd been bid to do. This was no different.

She'd climbed on the horse, attached her package as she'd been instructed, and ridden the beast straight to Lochluin Abbey. Once she'd arrived, she'd dismounted and handed the package over with only a few words exchanged. She'd been advised that Sister Matilda would be waiting for her.

Ever since then, the moment had haunted her but she'd never had anyone she dared to discuss it with. Had she done the right thing? And why had she been instructed to do what she had? What was the reason?

Did anyone know besides the four people involved?

She'd kept it a secret all these years, but it was time for her to let it go, tell someone, find out the true implications. Someone else had to know besides her. Maturity had settled on her shoulders, making her realize that others needed to know this secret.

Many years ago, she'd seen the nun's face, but had no idea what her name was. The sister had never told her who she was, just taken the package and hurried back inside.

The wee girl had been so confused, she hadn't known what to do. So she did the only thing she could do. She turned her horse around and returned home.

The sounds of approaching footsteps carried down the hall to her and her pulse quickened. Her palms sweat so much she feared the liquid would drip onto the floor. Wiping them down the tunic she wore helped a bit, but not much.

And what if the nun she'd met was no longer here? Then what would she do?

Her mind returned to the worn books in front of her. As she perused the titles, Tryana couldn't help but feel a sense of longing for her mother's voice and the memories of their time together. Flitting pictures of her beautiful mother flooded her mind, filling her with warmth and nostalgia. She remembered the many evenings spent with her mother, reading stories of magic and adventure. It was through these books that she had learned to dream, to imagine a different life. She had been so young then, and her mother had been taken from her far too soon. A tear rolled down her cheek as she remembered the last time she saw her mother, lying still and lifeless on her bed.

Lost in thought, Tryana didn't hear Sister Matilda's approach until she spoke. "Good day, my lady. You are waiting to see me? I am Sister Matilda. What can I do for you?"

Tryana wiped away her tears and stood up.

The nun's voice brought back so many emotions that she paused to take in everything about her, everything she recalled about that fateful day so long ago. Tryana peered at the woman closely and gasped. It was indeed the woman she'd given the package to many years ago. "Greetings, Sister Matilda. My name is Tryana de Gray. Might I have a word with you in private?"

The sister's shoulders fell and she hung her head for a moment, but then squared her shoulders and stared at her. "I know who you are, and I've been expecting you, Lady de Gray."

Tryana paused to gather the gumption to ask the question that had haunted her for years. She'd not leave until she gained the truth from the nun.

"Is my brother still alive?"

CHAPTER SIXTEEN

IT WAS A fierce but productive hunt for the Highlanders in the forest near Clan Cameron. Hoping for a deer, they had worked diligently to pick up the trail of a large animal, the kind to feed them all for a week.

And then Cadyn saw the dark hide in the underbrush.

He signaled to the others to be quiet and pointed in the direction of the animal. They crept forward silently, their hearts pounding with excitement. As they drew closer, the form of their prey came into view.

Heart racing, Cadyn raised his bow, its wood groaning under the pressure of his grip. He squinted, trying to make out the shape of the animal, but it was too well hidden. The only thing visible was the dark hide, and the occasional flash of an eye. Cadyn's breathing quickened as he steadied his aim, waiting for the perfect moment to strike.

Suddenly, the animal emerged from the underbrush, revealing itself to be a massive wild boar. Cadyn's heart skipped a beat as he realized the danger. This was no small animal, this was a beast of legend, larger than any boar he'd ever seen before.

The boar charged towards Cadyn, pounding the earth with its snout and tusks aimed straight at him. Cadyn's instincts took over and, with incredible reflexes, he dodged to the side, then fired his weapon. The boar crashed into a nearby tree, sending splinters flying in every direction.

Cadyn took advantage of the boar's distraction to notch an arrow and fire again, catching him in the flank.

The beast slowed, making odd sounds, but finally stopped in the middle of the group. Cadyn grinned when the boar finally fell, his arrow protruding from its side along with a smaller one. "Nice shot, Perrin!"

Aedan and Brin joined them, Aedan whistling when he saw the size of the wild pig they brought down. "Och, we'll be eating fine tonight and the morrow and fine stew after that. Glad ye will be staying for another day."

They gathered their prize up, tied its feet together and managed to get it back to the castle. They were surprised to see his sire and grandsire nearly at the gates.

"Logan Ramsay, ye old warrior, 'tis it truly ye I see in front of me? Jennie will be glad to see ye. And Cailean, I'm pleased ye came along with him. Yer son just got us a large boar for our supper this eve. I think we can start roasting it and have a hunk ready in time for dinner this eve. Ye'll join us?"

"Aye, and there are more coming. Wulf, Reyna, Isla, and Grif are at the stables. We caught up with them along the way. We sent the others with them back to Ramsay land since no one was in York. The baron is in the Highlands somewhere. They'll fill you in with the details."

"Terrific. We do have some news for ye. Tryana is safely with us, though her sire has not been seen. The baron has been found and his garrison sent back, but ye'll learn all inside. I'm overjoyed for this eve—great friends and good food. My favorite. I'll have to find a special drink or two for this eve. Mayhap a nice wine for us all." Aedan beamed with joy. "The monks often send some over, and I believe I have a cask saved."

By the time they arrived at the stables, the others had dismounted and were chatting at the gate. Wulf was waiting to hear the details, he guessed.

"Cadyn, where is my sister? Ye've found her, I hear?"

Cadyn replied, "We did find her. She was tied up by the baron, but he'll not be bothering her any longer."

"She is hale?"

"Aye, she slept in late this morn. She was exhausted. I'm sure she must be in the great hall. I'll go along with ye. Aedan is ready to take the meat out back to place on the pit."

Wulf took Reyna's hand and said, "Finally I'll get to see my sister, talk with her, see her smile again, I hope."

Cadyn led his sire and grandsire into the great

hall, Wulf and the others behind them. Jennie jumped out of her chair as easily as if she were but a new mother again. "Logan, I'm so pleased to see ye. I know ye dinnae travel as ye used to. What has brought ye here?"

His grandsire grumbled a bit without answering, but his father finally replied for him. "A headstrong grandson has him worried. Thinks he's no' thinking straight because there is a lass involved. 'Tis up to us to make sure he travels safely. But I hear the baron is already handled and Cadyn had a grand day hunting."

Maitland came in behind them, closing the door. "I knew ye couldnae stay away, Uncle Logan. Have a seat and I'll find ye a nice strong ale to hold ye through our story telling."

Wulf looked around the hall and asked, "May I ask where my sister is?"

Jennie said, "Dyna took her to Lochluin Abbey. She wished to speak with some of the older nuns, said her mother used to take her there. True?"

Wulf sighed and wrapped his arm around Reyna's waist. "Aye, 'tis true. We didnae live far from here and my mother used to sneak books out to read and to use to help teach us to read. She was clever about it because our sire wouldnae allow Tryana to learn because she was a lass."

Reyna and Isla broke into laughter in unison. "What a fool," Reyna said. "Why are some men so daft?"

"Daft or sneaky?" Wulf mumbled. "My sire is a fool but no' daft. I wish I knew where the hell he was."

The group spent about a quarter of the hour settling in around the hearth at the chair grouping and a nearby trestle table. Reyna asked Cadyn, "Where is Brin?"

"He's with his sire out back with the boar. There's a few with him."

She sat next to Cadyn and leaned over to whisper, "She is well?"

"Aye. He wished to whip her but we stopped it."

"Whip my sister?" Wulf bellowed loud enough to stop everyone in their tracks. "Who?"

"The baron," Maitland replied. "Worry not. We stopped him and handed him over to the local sheriff. And thank Cadyn for putting an arrow in his shoulder that forced him to drop the whip he was about to use on yer sister. Fine archery skills there. He ran like a wee lassie. Last I knew they were being escorted back to England and would be taken to the magistrate."

"He survived the arrow, I assume? 'Tis too bad in my eyes. Was my sire anywhere near him? I'd like to see an arrow in his arse. Or better yet, in his heart." Wulf stood, something Cadyn could understand. He was too upset about all that had taken place with his sister.

"The baron will survive the arrow to his shoulder, for certes, but he's being sent back to England. The worst is behind us," Cadyn said. "And as far as I know, no one has seen the second English garrison or yer sire. We took care of one. Maitland will tell ye all."

Wulf said, "Since we passed Lochluin Abbey on the way here, I think I will go find my sister before I do anything else. Ye all can save the details for me later." He reached for Reyna's hand. "I just need to see her sweet face. Do ye mind?"

"Nay, I'll go along with ye. 'Tis only a short ride and the day is lovely." The two took their leave while the rest of the group munched on bread and fruit from the kitchen.

Maitland filled them all in while Cadyn stepped out back to check on the boar. He didn't wish to be there to answer his grandsire's endless list of questions. It was better to let Maitland answer.

Brin said, "I see yer sire is here. Worried about ye?"

"Aye. I dinnae know who is worse, my sire or my grandsire. Have ye seen Tryana this morn?"

Brin shook his head. "I didnae see her but Papa did."

"Was she hale, Aedan? Did Jennie mention any new wounds appearing on her from the baron and her adventure in the forest?" He tried not to sound as concerned as he was, but since Wulf was going to meet her at the abbey, he wouldn't see her himself for a wee bit. He'd prefer to go galloping over to the abbey, but he wouldn't interrupt their reunion. Brother and sister needed some time alone.

Aedan said, "Jennie didn't mention anything, but I saw her riding with Dyna over to the abbey. I'm sure she is fine."

Cadyn nodded mindlessly. He wasn't sure of

anything. Would he be able to keep himself here until she returned?

Only for a short time.

Sister Matilda brought her into the library and said, "Please sit down, child. I will explain. Aye, your brother is still alive, and he has been living here with us. He is a fine lad, but he ran away. Brin sent a messenger to let me know that he is fine and with him, and I am guessing you already met Perrin." The nun closed the door and took the seat behind the desk.

"Perrin is my brother?"

"Aye. And there is more you should know. I am grateful you have come by because I did not wish to go to my grave," she paused to make the sign of the cross and a said a silent prayer, "... without telling the truth about all that happened back then. Wrath de Gray is an evil man, but I am sure you already know that."

A loud knock interrupted them. One of the other sisters answered the door but Wulf's voice came through strong and frantic. "My sister. Is she here? Is she safe?"

Tryana stood and said, "Pardon me, Sister, but I think I should show myself."

The nun folded her hands on the desk and waited. "As you wish."

Tryana opened the door and flew into her brother's arms. "I am fine, Wulf. I was saved from the baron, and I wish to never see him again."

He squeezed her tight but then stepped back. "The bas... He didnae hurt ye?"

"I am fine, but I must confess something I should have told ye long ago. Please join me in the library."

Wulf entered, Reyna at his side. They greeted the nuns kindly and moved into the library.

Sister Matilda asked Tryana, "He does not know all?"

"Nay," Tryana replied before taking a deep breath. "But I will tell all now."

Wulf looked from one face to the other, confused.

"Wulf, we have a brother."

He sat back in the chair and stared at her stupefied.

Sister Matilda said, "I'll step out while you tell your story. Then open the door and I'll join you. There is more to the story."

Once she left, Tryana turned to her brother and said, "I have a story to tell you. Please allow me to tell it all before you ask questions."

"I'm listening."

Reyna took his hand in hers.

CHAPTER SEVENTEEN

The home of Wrath de Gray, around eight years ago

TRYANA SAT AT the table, eating a piece of bread while she listened to her mother and father argue abovestairs.

Wulf came in and sat at the table with her. "What is happening?"

"Mama says she's about to have the wee bairn, so the maid went for the midwife."

"Why are they arguing?"

"I cannot overhear them. Did you hear anything when you came by?"

"I only heard Da say the words 'embarrass me.' I have no idea what that means." Her brother reached for a hunk of stale bread, gnawing on the thick crust.

Tryana had been nearly ten winters and Wulf six and ten. The two stared at each other as they often did when their parents argued.

Something that happened every single day of late. Papa would act furious, whisper words in her ear and Mama would sob, never saying anything to him.

Tryana vowed to be stronger than her mother when she grew up.

Wulf grabbed a hunk of cheese and some dried meat, then sat down, his hands wriggling as much as his feet bounced under the trestle table. Their home was small, but it did have two stories with three bedchambers abovestairs. The maid also did the cooking and stayed in a small chamber in the cellar. They never went hungry, but the happiness or smiles only took place when Wrath de Gray was gone.

The door opened and the midwife entered. She nodded to both of them and headed up the stairs. Wulf said to his sister, "I'm leaving for town. Da wanted me to go to market and get some ale for him. He already gave me the coin last eve. I dinnae wish to be here when Mama has the bairn."

"Godspeed," Tryana whispered as her brother headed out the door. She wished to beg him to stay, but she knew her brother's mind would not be swayed by her need for companionship.

But then he stuck his head back in the door and said, "Stay out of Papa's way. He gets mean when someone else is here. Ye know that." Her father insisted they speak like the English which is why Wulf liked to defy him and use his Scottish brogue when he wasn't around. She couldn't help but smile at her brother's defiant ways. And she loved the way he tried to protect her from their father and his many mood swings.

She would do as he said, knowing he was

correct. Whenever anyone else had to enter their home, Wrath became an even more cruel man, if that were possible. So she cleaned up the table, put everything in its place, donned her mantle, and headed outside. She'd rather feed the goats and the pigs.

It wasn't long before her father exited the small cottage and climbed on his horse, heading to market. He said nothing to her, and she was fine with that. She stepped back inside to see how the situation was going with the midwife. Having never had a younger brother or sister, or spent much time with a new bairn, she was excited about the babe. Mama had already taught her about putting raggies on the wee one, shown her the clothes she'd sewn.

She hoped it would be a wee sister to her, one with red locks.

Her mother let out a loud wail and Tryana started, a sudden fear of her mother dying shooting through her like a fire on a rooftop. One more yelp from her mother and she heard the quiet mews of the new bairn, something that made her smile.

Only a few moments later, the maid flew down the staircase with a basket in her hand, pushing it into Tryana's hands. "Take it."

She peeked into the basket and saw the wee bairn squirming and wiggling inside, a twisted piece of linen stuck in its mouth to suckle. "What? What shall I do with him? Or her?"

"'Tis a him and yer mother wishes him gone

before yer father and brother return. Tell no one but take the lad to Lochluin Abbey. There will be a nun there waiting for ye. Then hurry back."

Tryana asked, "We're giving the bairn to the nun?"

Her mother's voice called out to her. "Tryana, do as she says, or your sire will kill the bairn. Do it and tell no one. Hurry."

Kill the bairn? Her father would do such a thing?

She donned her mantle and grabbed the small basket lined and covered with warm plaids. The midwife instructed, "Take my horse. There is a handle on the saddle you can hang the basket on, just don't go too fast. You can be at the abbey in an hour."

She knew that much, and she understood the directions because she'd gone often before. Her mother liked to say her prayers and frequently attended chapel there. That was the place she'd learned to read and do her sums because her mother didn't want her father to know she could read. It was a beloved place to her.

But not to her father. He hated the abbey.

"Go, lass, and dinnae look back."

She quickly did as she'd been bidden and left, glad the weather was kind since it was a an early summer day. When she arrived at the abbey, she was surprised to see a nun run out to greet her. She took the basket, nodded and asked, "Lad or lassie?"

"Lad."

"Tell your mother we will take care of him."

That was the last time she ever saw her younger brother.

She'd never told her father or her older brother, but she was compelled to meet him now. And she hoped Wulf would forgive her.

CHAPTER EIGHTEEN

"FORGIVE ME FOR never telling you the truth, Wulf, but Mama made me promise."

Reyna said, "Ye were but ten years old. Ye were no' responsible."

Wulf stared up at the rafters in the library, his eyes misting. "And Mama lived only a few more days before the bastard pushed her down the stairs to her death." He let his breath out in a loud hiss.

Tryana stifled her tears. "I do not know why she did it. I never did, and I never came back to Lochluin Abbey until now to look for him."

The expression on her brother's face turned to one of hope. "We have a brother and he is alive?"

She nodded and moved over to open the door to let the nun know they were ready for her to return.

Sister Matilda came in and sat down behind the desk again. "So you know you have a brother, and he was raised here by us. He struggles because he has created a fantasy in his mind that his true father is an important man, a true warrior, and that he will return for him someday. We have done nothing to encourage this, but he persists. I think this is partly why he ran away."

"He ran away? We've lost him already?" Wulf barked.

"Nay," Tryana said. "I have met him, and he is with Brin at Cameron Castle. He is a sweet lad but he tells stories. He helped me when I escaped the baron, said his sire was Thor, but enough about that. Sister, you said there was more to the story. Please continue."

Wulf said, "I hope you can help us understand why our mother did this. I can't comprehend giving him away to be raised by nuns."

Sister Matilda folded her hands in her lap. "I can help you with that. Your mother was in love with someone else when she was forced to marry de Gray. She had fallen in love with your father a year before her parents betrothed her to de Gray. In fact, they handfasted. Wrath agreed to accept her as his wife because she was carrying you, Wulf, and her parents did not want her with your true father. They wished her to marry someone with noble blood so her father paid Wrath to marry her."

Wulf closed his eyes. "He was in debt and needed the coin. Always gambling."

"That is the way of it. You are aware of his faults. We hired the true father here, not knowing the situation at the time, but as we learned of it, we kept him here so he could watch over all of you. He was still in love with your mother. And since they had handfasted, we did not consider that they did anything wrong. You both have the blue eyes of your true father, someone who has passed on. He was a fine man who worked here as a carpenter for many years. He was a wonderful man who did whatever was needed of him, sometimes gardening or helping the monks. In fact, he was excited when Perrin was born and he came here to live, but alas, neither parent lived for long. It was our duty to raise your brother."

Sister Matilda cleared her throat and then continued, "Wrath was aware of her indiscretion. He became suspicious as you grew, Wulf, because you have the coloring of your true sire. He decided to punish your mother for this indiscretion. When you were born, Tryana, you were born a twin. Not identical, but you have a sister born on the same day and the same time as you."

"I do?" So stunned, those were the only words she could get out.

"To punish your mother, he took your sister away and hid her. And he promised never to return her until she gave him a son of his own. Thus Perrin was born, but your mother feared he had killed your sister, and she feared he would do the same with your brother Perrin, especially when she saw his blue eyes, so she sent him to us to protect him, knowing his true father was also here. Unfortunately, your sire died less than six months after Perrin was born. Some believe he died of a broken heart.

"Sending Perrin here was a simple act of a mother's love for her bairn. She did not want Wrath de Gray to ever meet him. He is not Perrin's sire either. We had hoped she would visit with him, but alas, she did not live long enough to ever see him again."

"And Wrath does no' know he lives?" Wulf asked.

"Nay, not to our knowledge. He has never inquired about him. But I would also like to add that the lad has been a delight to raise. He has a way of brightening our days here at the abbey. He is loved by many."

Tryana caught the misting of the older nun's eyes. She could easily see how one could love Perrin. "And my sister? Do you know where she lives? Where she is now? What her name is?"

"I'm sorry but we do not know the answer to that question. He used her existence to threaten your mother, but no one ever learned where she was. Your mother said her name was Ellen."

"I know where she is," Wulf declared, squeezing Reyna's hand.

"Where?" Tryana asked.

"Da…I mean Wrath owns a castle in Dulnain Valley. It is a dilapidated old castle but there was still one functioning tower. In fact, 'tis where they thought the baron was taking ye. He must have been taking ye to see Wrath. I dinnae know why, but 'tis what Maitland said they learned from the baron."

"Then we must go. We have a sister to save. Perrin will be fine until we return."

"But I dinnae know exactly where it is," Wulf said. "I'm unfamiliar with that part of the Highlands, and Dulnain Valley is a huge area. There are several inhabited castles there. Who could help us with that?" He looked to his wife for an answer.

Reyna replied, "Dyna. Clan Grant is near Dulnain Valley. Her sire knows everything about it. Perhaps we should seek him out. Alaric might be another one to ask."

The door to the abbey banged open and the chatter of a lad interrupted them. "Ladylana? Where are ye, Ladylana? I wished to see ye before ye left."

He hurried down the passageway as they stepped out into the hall. "Perrin," Sister Matilda called out. "Remember your manners and please come back here. Tryana is in the library and would like to speak with ye."

"She is hale?" he asked as he turned around and ran back toward the library. Then he stopped and whispered to the nun. "I punched her in the face by mistake, Sister. Please dinnae make me say penance for it. I dinnae mean it. It was an accident."

"Is that how her eye became bruised?" Sister Matilda asked.

"Aye, from me, and the baron too, but..."

"You may apologize to our Lord this eve in your prayers. I think He may forgive you under the circumstances. But come. I have something important to tell you."

Perrin stopped in front of her, folded his hands in front of him and asked, "Aye, Sister?"

"Come inside and I will tell you."

Perrin stepped into the large library and stared

at Tryana's face. "I knew it. Ye are bruised. Forgive me, Ladylana. I…"

"You were already forgiven, Magni. Please do not think on it again." Tryana fussed with his hair, a wide smile on her face. "And my true name is Tryana, not Ladylana."

He hung his head. "My name is no' Magni. I made it up. I wished to have a big father like Thor, one who would protect me and teach me how to use a sword and a hammer."

Tryana said, "That actually pleases me. I like your other name better, Perrin."

"My thanks for keeping my secret." He looked at Sister Matilda and said, "I ran away to the waterfall again, Sister. 'Tis where I met Tryana. My apologies."

Reyna said, "From what I heard, ye served a fine purpose at the waterfall. If no' for ye, Tryana may not have escaped the baron, even for the short time ye were together. I think Sister Matilda would agree that our Lord acts in odd ways sometimes. I think ye were meant to be there to help Tryana."

"Do ye think so, Sister?" He stared up at the nun with such hope that it squeezed Tryana's heart just a bit. This was her brother and she would do all she could for him.

"I do think He acts in ways we do not always understand, Perrin. Perhaps you were meant to help Tryana on her journey."

His quick smile was so beautiful that she reached over to squeeze Wulf's hand. They had a brother.

The nun placed her hand on the lad's shoulder. "Perrin, I have something important to tell you, so please listen carefully. Tryana is your sister and this man's name is Wulfstan. He is your brother, and this is his wife, Reyna. You have a family now."

His eyes widened. "I do? Ye are my brother?"

Wulf nodded and said, "I've always wished for a brother. My wish has been granted. I'll teach ye how to use a sword like Thor."

He spun to face Tryana. "And ye are my sister?"

"Aye, does that not please you? It pleases me verra much because we can be a family together. You won't have to live here any longer. You can live with us."

"But where do ye live?" he asked, looking at Reyna.

"We live on Ramsay land for now."

"Where do ye live, Tryana?"

She looked at her brother, her eyes misting, and said, "I don't know. I do not have a home at present."

"Then you can live on Ramsay land with us," Wulf said. "We'll be a family. Ye and Perrin and the two of us can be together."

Perrin looked at both of them and then screamed, "Nay, ye'll leave me there where I dinnae know anyone. Ye'll desert me like my mother did. I'm no' goin'! I'd rather stay here."

Perrin ran out of the library and down the passageway toward the back of the abbey just as a knock sounded at the front door.

Wulf took off after him.

CHAPTER NINETEEN

CADYN TRUSTED THAT all was well with Tryana, but he wished to set his own eyes on her. His feelings for the lass were growing in different ways, something he was unsure of, but he was always pleased to see her, and he had a powerful sense of protection when it came to the beautiful lass. So he made his way to the abbey, hoping to find her inside. He ran into Dyna on her way from the stable to the abbey.

"Tryana is here?" he asked.

"Aye, I came here with her, but she's been speaking with the nun for a while and Wulf is here, so I think I'll take my leave. I know ye will gladly escort her back. True, Cadyn?" Dyna waggled a brow at him.

Uncertain how to respond, he said, "Of course. I'll gladly return with her."

Dyna stayed him with a touch of her hand to her forearm. "But she's more than a lass who needs yer protection. Correct? I dinnae mean to embarrass ye but I think the two of ye make a lovely match. She needs someone strong and steady in her life, and that man is ye, Cadyn."

Still confused, he said, "My thanks. I'm no' sure how I feel, if that makes sense."

"Makes perfect sense," Dyna chided. "I hated Derric Corbett and loved him at the same time. Talk about making me daft. Just relax and take the relationship as it comes. Ye are in a tough situation because of her betrothal, but I believe it will all work out." They made it to the door and she knocked.

A different nun answered the door and let Dyna and Cadyn in, and they were able to see Tryana seated in the library. "There ye are. We were just checking on ye," Dyna explained. "I'm leaving in a few more moments, but Cadyn is here so he will escort ye back, lass."

Cadyn said, "I'll be happy to do so."

Dyna looked at the faces that stepped out of the library and said, "Ye all look like ye've seen a ghost. My mother will tell ye odd things can happen in an abbey."

Tryana was visibly upset. "Excuse me, I must go find Perrin. And Cadyn can escort me back. Do as you wish, Dyna."

Reyna ushered Dyna and Cadyn into the library and quickly explained all while Tryana tapped her foot, clearly ready to go after the lad. Cadyn remarked, "He's yer brother. That should please him, I would expect. I think he is just absorbing it all."

Wulf returned alone, shrugging his shoulders. "The lad is quick-footed. I tried to catch up with him, but he's disappeared. Where is his chamber, Sister? Or should I look for him outside?"

Sister Matilda placed her hand on Wulf's arm. "The poor lad just received a shock. I'm sure he's afraid you will both leave him. Perrin runs to his chamber occasionally, but also runs out the door too. But he also has quite a bit of energy. Sometimes, he prefers to run outside where he can be loud and not be chastised."

Tryana kneaded her hands. "But he ran away to the waterfall. Where else would he go?"

"He's only run away to Cameron Castle and the waterfall. He's never gone any farther, and that is a rare occurrence. I would wager he is running in circles on the hill behind the abbey. He is probably there now so I'll speak with him. Allow me some time with him and send Brin. He's verra fond of him, treats him like a brother. Perhaps it would be best if he spoke with someone he trusts first."

Dyna said, "That makes sense, Sister. I'll go find Brin. Perrin seemed verra fond of him. If I am unable to find him, I will return to let ye know."

The older nun took her leave and headed down the passageway after the lad.

Wulf said, "So much has happened. I'm just absorbing this all too. I'd like to go back to Cameron hall and ask for some advice. We just learned we have a sister, but we don't know how to find her. I'm thinking the elders of the clan could help us. And I have questions for ye, Dyna, but I'll save them for Cameron hall."

Cadyn moved over to Tryana and said, "Ye must be shocked as well. I'll escort ye back."

Reyna said to the other nun, "We will take our leave. Please let Sister Matilda know that we will send Brin back to talk with Perrin and hope they will come for supper this eve."

They filed out of the abbey and over to the stable where their saddled horses grazed leisurely near the trees. Cadyn helped Tryana to mount, then climbed up behind her.

Tryana said, "My thanks for allowing me to ride with ye. I'll be leaving my horse here. Will they return it? I just am so upset I don't trust myself."

Dyna overheard and said, "They exchange horses all the time. Dinnae worry."

Once they headed back, Cadyn said, "Ye must be exhausted, lass."

"I am," she said, leaning back against him. "But I am too confused to sleep. I just learned I have a sister, yet I have no idea how to find her. Wulf will speak with Dyna and Alaric, see if they can help us because he believes Wrath owns a castle not far from Grant land."

They didn't talk much on the way back, Cadyn busy trying to process everything Tryana and Wulf had just learned. They had a brother and a sister. He couldn't help but wonder how this had all been accomplished by their father. He let her relax against him, enjoying this small intimacy they shared. Tryana's scent pleased him, and the silkiness of her hair drove him to thoughts he tried to suppress but failed.

Visions of the lass with her hair down came to him.

What was happening to him? He was on a mission assigned to them by King Robert. Why was he so distracted?

They reached Cameron land in no time, the group arriving at the stables and dismounting quickly. Cadyn said, "Dyna, we'll explain everything to Brin." Cadyn led Tryana around behind the castle where the boar was being roasted and gave Brin his message.

"I'll go speak with him." Brin agreed quickly. "Tell me why ye think he is upset before I go."

Tryana told him about their meeting with the nun, and Brin said, "My thanks for the explanation. He will be fine once he thinks on it. I'm sure it was a surprise. He likes ye, Tryana, so I'm sure he will accept ye as his sister. And just to let ye know, I'm pleased for him. Ye and Wulf will be good for him. Growing up on Ramsay land is a fine place, so I'll talk with him about that. He has no idea what Ramsay land is."

"Many thanks to ye, Brin."

Brin left and the rest of the group went inside. He brought Tryana to the table his sire and grandsire sat at, introducing her to both of them.

Tryana said, "It is a pleasure to meet you both but I must excuse myself. I see my brother across the hall and would like to speak with him before he leaves." Turning to Cadyn, she gave a small smile and said, "Thank you for escorting me back from the abbey."

"It was my pleasure, lass. Go speak with Wulf now and I will look for you later," Cadyn promised.

She left and headed to the far side of the hall where Wulf and Reyna sat with Isla and Grif.

Cadyn turned back to his sire and grandsire.

"How long are ye here for? Was there a point to this visit?"

His sire said, "We have no' been to Cameron land in a while, so just thought to visit. See if ye were in any need of our help."

His grandsire let out a small snort. "And to see that Cadyn does no' do anything foolish, like chase off on his own to save a lass."

Cadyn couldn't believe his ears. "We did save her but it was a group of us. Why would ye think I would go off on my own? I need help with a garrison of a score of Englishmen."

"I'm glad of it. Pleased to see ye used a good plan. And proud of ye for sticking the bastard in the shoulder. Mama and Grandmama will love to hear it." His father had a wide grin on his face.

"Grandsire? Will ye trust me now?"

The man actually snorted again. "Nay."

Cadyn stood up. "Why the hell no'?"

His grandfather said, "Because I recall what 'twas like to be smitten by a lass. I did foolish things, but I was verra lucky. I dinnae wish to see ye do the same."

"Ye helped Grandmama, did ye no'?" Cadyn declared louder than he should of.

"Aye, but I was wiser then than ye are."

Cadyn threw his hands up in the air and walked away, moving out to the fire pit where the boar was roasting. He had to get away from it all.

Aedan approached him and said, "I know that look. Upset with yer sire or grandsire, lad?"

"My grandfather. He treats me like a bairn. Always trying to guess what I'm going to do, and then telling me no' to do it. He's always harping at me, one way or the other. I have to walk away sometimes."

"'Tis the best way to handle it. Yer grandfather is a wise man, an experienced man who knows how to upset everyone. But he also can be quite resourceful when it comes to problems. Ye'll see someday, but I'm sure he's a wee bit overprotective. Though I'm sure ye recognize that he holds the most concern for those who mean the most to him."

Cadyn cast him a sideways glance. While Aedan was probably correct, it never felt like he was concerned for him. Only that he liked to make Cadyn's life a daily challenge. "Bosses me around everywhere. I thought he might leave me be now that I'm in with Maitland's and Dyna's group."

"He does no' trust the English. This is a bad situation. He lived most of his life under King Alexander III who kept peace with the English. As a spy for the Scottish Crown, he learned more than he wanted to about how low the English will sink when it comes to the Scots. Everything has changed now with King Alexander gone and King Edward, and 'tis for the worse."

"I suppose ye are right."

"Stay back here, Cadyn. 'Tis oft better to let yer grandsire stew on his own. Maitland is headed this way, and I'm going to speak with Jennie about dinner. Brin should be back soon too." He clasped Cadyn's shoulder and left just as Maitland stepped outside. Their conversation was mostly light, but then Maitland said, "I'm hoping Wulf will keep things peaceful until after supper. The twin sister has been hidden for a long time. I dinnae think one more day will matter. We'll search for her on the morrow. Until then, we all deserve a good meal and some laughter. Do ye no' agree, Cadyn?"

"I do."

Maitland moved over to talk with another group while Cadyn made his way around to the front of the castle. He decided to go brush his dear horse down. He found the stables peaceful.

Only three stable lads were inside, while two guards manned the gates, but it was set to be a quiet eve. Dusk would be here soon. He took care of his own horse, then moved to his father's and his grandfather's.

All was well for about an hour before a frantic voice called out to him.

Brin arrived breathless on horseback from the abbey.

"What's wrong?" he asked Brin.

Brin cursed. "Perrin ran away, and I cannae find him anywhere. I'm calling for some help."

Hellfire.

Here we go again.

CHAPTER TWENTY

TRYANA HAD ALMOST made it to the stable when Brin arrived. She overheard Brin's comment and raced over to stand next to Cadyn. "He's gone? Are you sure?"

"I cannae find him anywhere. I'm going to the waterfall next. We found that cave together, and I know he loves it there."

"Aye," Tryana said. "That is where I met him. He does love it there. I'll go with you."

Cadyn said, "I'll go along with ye."

Brin spoke to the guards. "I'll take four of ye with me. It will no' take long to find the cave so we should be back in less than an hour."

Wulf came up to them. "We'll go with ye."

Brin said, "Many thanks, but I fear ye may have frightened Perri away. Please stay here or patrol in this area. I may never get him out of that cave if ye are there, Wulf. He's a young lad and confused. He'll adjust to ye and love ye in no time at all. Too much has happened to a lad who spent most of his time helping the nuns or visiting me. His life was verra quiet until he met Tryana."

"Also probably why he ran away," Wulf said. "While it goes against my gut, I see yer point."

Reyna said, "We will make him a fine home with yer sister."

Wulf grumbled, "I know. Go, the three of ye will have a better chance without me."

They left immediately, the seven of them, heading straight toward the cave. Tryana was glad Brin led the way because she had no idea how to get there. Her directions were not the best. Her brother had often made fun of how she attempted to go in the wrong direction time and again. Not this time. It was not one of her strengths.

She rode with Cadyn, something she was growing to like more and more. He held her tight around the waist when they hit rough spots in the road, but otherwise let her decide how to sit best. Her favorite was to lean against him, take in his heat, his quiet strength, and his scent. He always had the aroma of pine and mint wafting round him, something quite pleasing to her.

It was nearly dark when they arrived at the waterfall. She began yelling for him as soon as they arrived, but they received no answer.

Brin dismounted and said, "Ye were in the cave with him, Tryana?"

"Aye."

"Then ye should go first. Be alert to anything that looks different. That would prove that he has been here. From what he told me, he left as soon as ye were taken so everything should be undisturbed."

Cadyn dismounted from his horse, offering his

hand to Tryana to help her down. She took it, relishing the warmth of his hand as he pulled her to the ground. Together they made their way to the waterfall, their footsteps drowned out by the melodious sound of water against the rocks.

Tryana shivered, the chill of the damp area seeping into her bones. Cadyn noticed and wrapped his arm around her, pulling her closer to his side. She leaned into him, grateful for his warmth.

Brin came from behind them, scanning the area for a lost lad, but he was not there. The group made their way toward the cave, the sound of the waterfall growing louder as they approached. Tryana's heart sank as they found the entrance to the cave empty. There was no sign of her brother or anyone else. She looked around in confusion, wondering if they had somehow missed him on the way there.

As she turned to face the group, she caught Cadyn's eye and saw the worry etched in his expression. He took her hand in his and gave it a reassuring squeeze.

"We'll find him," he said firmly. "We won't stop until we do."

Tryana nodded, feeling a small glimmer of hope begin to form in her chest. She trusted Cadyn more than anyone else in the world, and if he said they would find her brother, then she believed him.

As they began to search the cave, they moved cautiously, wary of any potential danger lurking in the shadows.

Brin took a torch from one of his guards and she moved behind the waterfall and into the cave, the three of them together while she called out to Perrin.

But it was not to be. Once inside the area with the light, she glanced around and said, "There is nothing different. I do not believe he has been here. His extra arrows have not been moved, and neither has his plaid on the rock. It looks exactly the same."

The three stood in the middle of the small cave mystified. "Where would he go? Any other ideas?" Cadyn asked.

"Nay," Tryana said. "What say you, Brin?"

"This was my best guess. We hunted in many places, but this is the only place we went to often. His other favorite places were the royal burghs. He liked to eat and go through the merchant stalls, but there is nowhere close that he could visit at night. He didnae take a horse, so he is traveling on foot."

Brin led the way back out into the forest.

Cadyn followed behind Tryana. "Brin, I hate to ask this but do ye think it would be possible he would have been kidnapped by reivers for any reason? Have ye any unsavory groups around of late?"

"Not lately. And he knows he must be wary."

Tryana couldn't calm her worry, her hands kneading in front of her. "But he was not thinking clearly. He was too busy trying to absorb that he had a new family. Though I know not why that would upset him. I thought he would be pleased about it."

Cadyn helped her onto his horse, then said, "It may only be because of change. He knows everything in his life is about to transform."

"But he ran away to the cave and told lies about his father."

"I think Cadyn is correct," Brin said. "He wanted a family, but in turn, he probably hadn't thought about the fact that he would have to leave the abbey and Cameron land. He's verra fond of my aunt and uncle, of my sire…"

"And you," Tryana said. "You've been wonderful with him, Brin."

"I'm attached to him, as well. I'll no' rest until we find him. I think we need to head back while there is still a wee bit of light. I'm hoping they found him hiding somewhere."

Tryana prayed he was right.

They were back before she knew it, but she could tell Perrin hadn't returned. Brin yelled to the guards at the gate, "Has Perrin been found?"

"Nay. Wulf and Reyna are back at the abbey talking with Ruari. They'll be back soon."

Brin said, "Then we need to go inside and plan our next step. We have plenty of men to help us, fortunately."

Brin hurried inside while Cadyn helped Tryana to dismount. As soon as her feet hit the dirt, he tugged her in close for a hug, his chin resting on the top of her head.

"I cannot lose the brother I just found, Cadyn." She fought the tears but stayed in his warm embrace. It felt wonderful to have someone she trusted nearby.

"Dinnae worry. We will find him. Come, ye will be getting a chill. Warm up by the fire, at least." He kept his arm around her, holding her close, escorting her to the door.

Once inside, there were so many people talking that she said, "I'm going to change clothes. I'll be right back down."

She hurried up the stairs, wanting to get out of the now dirty leggings she'd worn in the cave. She had another pair Jennie had found for her so she would don them and return to find out what the plan would be.

Inside her chamber, she found a piece of parchment on the pillow on her bed. Scowling, she moved over to pick it up, read it quickly, then dropped it with a short squeal.

Tryana,

I know you can read this, so do not show it to anyone else. I have your brother, the one you whisked away from me many years ago. And I know where your sister is. I will be sending two men to escort you to me. Be outside the back curtain wall behind the pit when the sun drops.

If you tell anyone, I'll kill Perrin. Come alone.

Wrath de Gray

She changed her clothes, tucked a dagger inside the convenient fold in her tunic made by Gwyneth Ramsay, and snuck down the back staircase, making sure that no one saw her.

She'd kill Wrath de Gray if she had to.

CHAPTER TWENTY-ONE

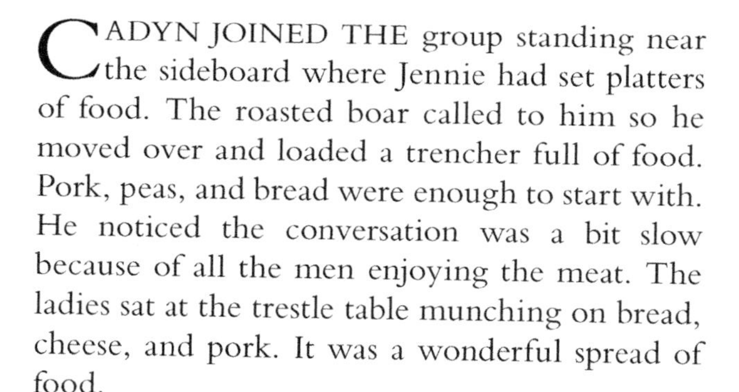

CADYN JOINED THE group standing near the sideboard where Jennie had set platters of food. The roasted boar called to him so he moved over and loaded a trencher full of food. Pork, peas, and bread were enough to start with. He noticed the conversation was a bit slow because of all the men enjoying the meat. The ladies sat at the trestle table munching on bread, cheese, and pork. It was a wonderful spread of food.

The teasing started. "Hurry, Cadyn," Maitland said. "'Tis nearly gone. Ye better hurry."

He said it with a gleam in his eye but Cadyn ignored him. "Have ye heard anything about Perrin?"

"Nay," Dyna replied. "Wulf and Reyna went to the abbey to check there. Ye saw no sign of him by the waterfall?"

"None," he said between bites. "Where could he have gone?"

His grandfather said, "We dinnae know, but please dinnae run off after him without some guards."

"Grandda, why do ye always think the worst of me?" If he'd had a chicken leg in his hand, he would have tossed it at the old goat.

"I dinnae, I just know ye have yer eyes on that lass and that makes ye do foolish things."

His sire cut in, "He has good judgment, Logan. Leave him be. Let him eat in peace. He's been busy this day."

Grandda snorted then headed out the back door.

Cadyn finished his meal quickly and excused himself from the table, making his way towards the stables. He needed a break from all the chattering and gossiping. As he walked, he couldn't help but think about Perrin. The lad had been missing for hours now, and no one seemed to know where he had gone. Cadyn could feel his pulse quicken at the thought of his being hurt or in danger.

He reached the stables and entered, inhaling the familiar scent of hay and horses. His gaze landed on his mare, and he made his way to her stall, stroking her nose as he spoke soothingly to her.

"Perrin's missing," he whispered to the mare, as if she would understand. Raven nickered in response, and Cadyn felt a sense of comfort wash over him.

He knew he had to do something, and he couldn't wait for the others to come up with a plan. But a sudden realization hit him like the cold water of an autumn loch. Tryana had not returned. Reminding himself that she could be taking care of her needs besides changing her clothes, he gave her a few more minutes, then crept up the back staircase from the outside, hoping to go unnoticed.

The door to her chamber was open so he rapped lightly, then stuck his head into the door. "Tryana?"

No answer. He stepped into the chamber, taking in all the details as his grandsire had taught him. She had changed her clothing because her worn leggings lay in a heap on the bed. He perused the rest of the chamber for some clue, then he saw it.

A piece of parchment lay on the floor, folded in two.

He read the missive, then cursed because he knew she'd done something foolish. She'd gone outside without telling anyone, wanting to make sure no one would follow her.

Cadyn knew her well enough to know that she would not risk anyone else's life. He had to hurry to catch her.

He had a wee niggling in the back of his mind about the conversation they'd just had, but the only thing he was willing to do was throw the missive into the passageway to be sure it would be found.

His father, his grandfather, Brin, Wulf, Maitland, Dyna—they'd all be following.

That was too risky. He had to snort on the way down the back staircase. Seems his grandsire was right about him after all. He couldn't risk losing Tryana.

He hoped to make her his wife someday. That thought came with nearly the same feeling as his grandda smacking the back of his head.

Racing down the back staircase, he snuck out through the back door in the curtain wall, but then he cursed.

He was too late. He could see the dust stirred up from the three horses, but he had no chance of catching them on foot. Instead, he ran around to the front to the stable, glad to see the gate was open. "Saddle my horse," he yelled to the stable lad while he ran to fill a sack with some apples, oatcakes, a dagger, and an extra plaid he took from the shelf. Then he grabbed extra arrows from the big barrel, found his sword, and bow. Mounting quickly, he said to the stable lad, "When they come looking for me, tell them I went after Tryana. There's a missive abovestairs that will explain all."

"Did I cause trouble?" the stable lad yelled. "A man came along and said to place the missive in the place where Tryana slept. I gave it to one of the maids."

Cadyn yelled at him, "No problem. I will find her."

Then he left, sending his mount into a full gallop across the meadow, cutting across a small glen to catch up to Tryana. He'd have to stay back, use his tracking skills, and wait until he could save her. He couldn't risk letting her captors see him.

The sun was setting, casting the sky in shades of orange and pink, and he knew that time was running out. He had to act fast before it was too late.

As he rode, the wind whipped through his hair, and his heart pounded with fear for Tryana's safety. He couldn't believe that she had been taken, and he cursed himself for not being able to protect her.

They had to find Perrin and her sister. The others would be along in no time. Of that much he was certain.

But he also had another thought. He and Dyna had both been correct.

Tryana was near a waterfall and her sister was in a tower. His dream had been true.

Tryana never spoke to the two men who escorted her to wherever her sire awaited her. They traveled for at least four hours in the middle of the night, though they fortunately had a full moon on a cloudless night. Otherwise, she'd have had no idea where she was.

Hours passed, and Tryana's anxiety only grew. She was hungry, thirsty, and scared. She tried to stay calm, but the silence was deafening.

They headed north, so she guessed her brother was correct about Wrath, the man she refused to call her father ever again, having a castle in the Highlands. So weary that she wished to sleep, she didn't dare for fear of falling off her horse. They'd tied her hands together and one man held onto the reins of her mare, leading her through the path in the Highlands.

After seeing the mountains in the distance, she knew they were headed north.

"How much farther?" she asked, afraid she would fall soon.

"One more hour. You can hold it until then."

One man looked at the other and said, "Have ye known Wrath much?"

The second man said, "Nay, just met him for this. Will he pay us fairly?"

First man said, "Och, he'll pay, but if ye dinnae do what he says, he'll take it out in yer hide." He glanced back at Tryana and said to second man, "It couldnae have been easy being his daughter. The question is where did he take his anger out on ye, lassie? On yer back or yer sweet arse?" Then he chuckled while the second one guffawed.

Tryana ignored the two but listened to every word.

"Are ye staying after we get her there?" the second asked.

"Aye, he paid me to stay. If I were ye, I'd take yer coin and run. He gets in a mood and he willnae pay ye."

Amused by their uncertainty, she couldn't help but speak her mind. "And what if he's a dead man? Will he pay you your coin then?"

They both laughed until first man asked, "What makes ye think ye can kill him?"

She pursed her lips and stared up at the stars in the sky. "I will not kill him. But you probably did not pay much attention to where you took me from and who else was there, did you?"

"It was near an abbey. I dinnae fear any monks." This was the second man's wisdom.

"It was Cameron Castle and it was full of Ramsays and Grants. You have heard of Logan Ramsay, have you not?"

First man glanced at second man with a frown. "Ramsay?"

Second man said, "I've heard of that Connor Grant. He's huge and fierce. They say he's the finest swordsman in all the land."The two glanced at each other, doubt entering their eyes as clearly as if they'd spit on the ground.

"Do you know Logan's wife, Gwyneth Ramsay? Or what about Dyna Corbett, daughter of Connor Grant? Or Maitland Menzie. Or mayhap Wulfstan de Gray and his wife Reyna. She's from Clan Matheson. Not far from here. Gwyneth Ramsay's daughters and granddaughters were there too. They were all there and they'll be coming for me."

"Shut yer mouth," first man said, spinning around.

Second man whispered, "Who is she speaking of? I dinnae know any of those names but the Grants."

"The Ramsay woman has a reputation. Her husband is Logan Ramsay, and she's the best archer in all the land."

"The beast of the Highlands? That Logan Ramsay?" His face paled even in the moonlight.

Now Tryana smiled. "And their grandson is on his way along with all the others I just named. They'll wait until I approach my sire alone, but you can be sure they will show up." She had to admit that playing with these men's fears was quite entertaining.

"Gwyneth Ramsay. Mayhap I've heard of her.

Why?" second man said to himself as much as anyone. He scratched his head.

"I'll tell ye, fool," first man said. "She's the one who pinned Bearchun to a tree by the bollocks."

"Why the hell did ye not tell me what clan we were going to? We're dead men if they catch us," second man grumbled.

"It was by an abbey. How would I know the Grants and Ramsays would be there? We'll get out ahead of them. Ye'll see."

Tryana grinned as the two men fidgeted.

The second one nearly fell off his horse but the first one saved him. "Wake up. We drop her off, get our coin and run before anyone follows."

"That should work," she reasoned. "As long as you are sure no one is behind us following now. They are expert trackers so they know how to follow without being seen."

Both men spun around to check behind them but no one was there. They faced forward again and urged their horses to go faster.

Tryana leaned forward and whispered, "I can sense them. They are not far behind."

They both whirled around to stare at her but she only did one thing.

She grinned.

CHAPTER TWENTY-TWO

WULF AND REYNA stopped at the stables, dismounting quickly. "Any word about Perrin?" Wulf asked the stable lad.

"Nay, but Cadyn left and said to tell ye there is a note in the passageway abovestairs that ye all need to read."

"What?" Wulf asked.

"Oh, and he said he was going after Tryana." The lad looked up at Wulf earnestly as if he carried the secret of the world.

Indeed he did.

"How long ago did he leave?" Wulf asked. "Who was with him?"

"Half the hour, my lord. And he was alone. Took his bow, a dagger, and his sword."

Reyna said, "Come. We must go abovestairs and find that note. Something is amiss for certes." She had that feeling, that unsettled feeling had come over her on the way back from the abbey as if something were happening that she needed to know about.

They stepped inside the hall and noticed nothing unusual happening. Reyna strode over to her grandfather. "Grandda, yer grandson and Tryana are missing and ye have no' noticed?" Then she spun around and followed Wulf up the staircase hoping they'd find the missive.

Her words had unsettled the group below. Clearly they'd been more interested in the food than with Cadyn.

Brin took the stairs three at a time. "Ye have heard something."

Reyna found the missive and picked it up. She glanced at her husband, knowing that this would feel like a knife to his belly. "'Tis from Wrath. Says he is holding Perrin and Ellen and that Tryana is to come alone."

Wulf nearly ran down the steps, but she grabbed his arm, staying him. "My sire always says get all the information first. Listen, Wulf. Please."

He closed his eyes as she led him over to the balcony overlooking the hall. "I have an announcement." Then she let out a shrill whistle and everyone stopped to stare at them, her grandfather moving toward the balcony.

Reyna read the note, then said, "We have no' seen him, but the stable lad said Cadyn left half an hour ago, and he is going after Tryana."

"He left alone?" Grandda bellowed. "After I told him no' to? I'll kill him."

Reyna leaned over the railing and shouted back at him, "First we have to find him, Grandda. And whether ye know this or no', he's trying to save the woman he loves. If we all went with him, we'd have been seen. He did the right thing and ye know it."

Grandda grumbled but then crossed his arms and smiled. "Hellfire, but the lad did do the right thing."

Reyna shook her head and yelled, "Maitland and Dyna, ye decide how to divide us up, but Wulf and I will be at the stables. Give ye a few moments to decide. We should all be ready to go in less than a quarter hour."

Wulf squeezed her hand and tugged her down the stairs behind him. Her grandfather began shouting and Dyna shouted, "Uncle Logan, Maitland and I know the group best. We'll decide."

Grandda mumbled again but then smiled at Reyna with pride as she flew down the staircase. "Ye've done good too, lassie. Ye make me a proud old man. Now go find them."

Reyna grinned as she followed Wulf out the door. Her grandfather was turning soft. "Wulf, we'll find them."

The group fell out of the keep all chattering. Dyna said, "Alaric, ye and I know Dulnain Valley best. Ye go with Maitland to the northeast and I'll take southwest. If I find there is a huge garrison, I'll stop and get Da to mount up a group to help us."

Alaric said, "My da would love to help."

Once outside the curtain wall, the stable lads hurried to saddle all the horses, but everyone helped. Reyna said, "We're going with Dyna as soon as ye have the group ready."

Wulf said, "I feel like I need to race off. Push my horse until we are there."

Reyna said, "We cannae be ahead of Cadyn. Let him follow them. Remember Wrath's words. If we follow Tryana, he'll kill them. Cadyn was trained by Grandmama and Grandda. He is truly one of our best, but no one gives him the chance. I promise ye, he'll know exactly where yer sire is."

Dyna added, "This fits with our dreams. I saw Tryana near the waterfall, but he saw her in the tower. *Ellen* is in the tower. Our dreams say it is so. Cadyn was so close."

Reyna squeezed her husband's hand, "Remember, he said he'll kill Perrin if he sees any of us. Ye believe he would do it, Wulf?"

Wulf helped her to mount, then found his own horse. "Aye, he would do it in a moment. He'd love to pay her back for leaving the baron again. I'm sure word reached him quickly."

Reyna led Wulf out to the spot to wait. Dyna joined them with Brin, Ceit, Dobbin, and Tevis. Brin yelled for five Cameron guards to join them.

The other group gathered, but Dyna said, "We dinnae need to wait for them. Time to go. We just have to find Cadyn, so look for any sign of him and we follow."

Reyna said, "This time, if we find Wrath, Wulf, put your sword through his black heart. If ye dinnae, I'll put an arrow in it."

Tryana said nothing as they approached a dilapidated old castle, though she had no idea where they were. She prayed she would indeed find Perrin was safe, even if he was here. There was no doubt in her mind that Wulf, Reyna, Cadyn, and the others would soon follow.

She couldn't tell them when she left for fear her sire would carry out his threat. This was the correct way. Once she managed to get inside, she'd find out where Perrin was, and perhaps even meet the sister she hadn't known she'd had.

Ellen. A fine English name. Wrath de Gray was always trying to get rid of everything inside of them that made them Scottish. He wanted them to become English, eliminate every touch of their mother from them.

Never. Not in her mind. She'd teach Ellen how kind their mother was.

Her next thought made her wonder where Ellen had been brought up. Perrin had been raised at the abbey by the nuns and the monks. All kind people. But what of Ellen? Where had she lived her entire life? Clearly not with Wrath.

The men dismounted, then pulled her off her horse, catching her before she fell forward since her hands remained tied, preventing her the opportunity to maintain her balance.

First man said, "We get her inside, collect our coin, then leave. Agreed?"

"Aye," second man answered. "I have no desire to stay here and wait for the Ramsays to arrive. We arenae far from Grant land either. I dinnae know if he's aware of that or no'. Was he ever here? Does he live here?"

First man shrugged. "I know naught. I heard of the chance to gain good coin. Here I am, but now I know she's tied to the Ramsays and Grants,

I'm out. I like to live. The two Grant brothers and their sons all scare the hell out of me. Have ye ever seen how tall they are? The two dark-haired ones look like warriors from the north. Massive shoulders, taller than anyone I've ever seen. And the one named Alasdair has no fear, so they say. And their sword skills...unbelievable." He tugged her along next to him and said to the other man. "We need to make this exchange and be quick about it."

"I hope they have other guards here because I'm no' staying either."

The two continued to look back over their shoulder. Each time they did, she giggled to herself.

"Stop yer laughing," first man said.

"Your fear is warranted. I've seen the patrol of King Robert's best men from Clan Grant and Clan Ramsay. Ye should be afraid. They will definitely be following me."

"Shut yer mouth."

Wrath de Gray appeared suddenly, stopping all their conversation. "You let a woman's simple mind bother you? She's a fool. Ignore her."

"We did as ye asked and have no' been followed. I'll take my coin and leave. I have another job lined up." First man shoved her toward Wrath.

Second man nodded. "Same for me."

"Get the hell out." He handed them their coin.

First man said, "Ye said double."

"Double if you stay. You said you're leaving."

Both men looked at their coin, then at her, then whirled around and left.

She didn't wait to go after Wrath. "Where are Perrin and my sister?"

He grabbed her by the elbow and propelled her in front of him. "You'll see soon enough." He put his lips close to her ear as they walked, his voice coming out with such disdain that she could feel it. "I've learned you are the one who stole my son away from me. You put him in a basket and took him to the nuns. You were seen leaving my house while I was gone. Someone finally came forward and told me. It cost me some coin, but it was worth it to learn that you were the one who took away all my hope for a son. Because *you* are the guilty party, you will be punished, justifiably so."

"Guilty? I was ten years old, Wrath."

"Father. I am your father." He gripped her upper arm so tight that she knew he would leave a bruise.

"Nay, you are not. You killed my mother and for that I will never forgive you. You are a cruel, vindictive man who will never be happy. You could have ten doting bairns and you would not be happy."

He slapped her hard, and with her hands tied, she had no recourse but to take the blow and duck her chin to protect herself from another. But it gave her a sweet satisfaction that her words had stung, had hit him in a vulnerable place. "Where is Perrin?"

He said nothing, instead shoving her forward toward a crumbling keep that looked deserted. "Perrin! Where are you?"

She screamed her brother's name, but the only

response she received was the echo of her own voice bouncing off the walls of the deserted keep. As she stumbled forward, she couldn't help but think back on the events that had led her to this moment.

Her father, the man who had just slapped her and held her captive, had always been a cruel and vindictive person. Her mother had paid the ultimate price for defying him, and her brother had been kept from her ever since.

But she had not given up hope. Her brother was out there somewhere, and she would find him, no matter the cost. And now she'd learned there was a sister out there too. What sweet irony for her.

As she approached the keep, she saw movement out of the corner of her eye. Cadyn. She would not let on that she'd seen anyone. First, she had to learn where Perrin and Ellen were being kept. She tripped on the stairs, but righted herself, hoping to draw attention away from Cadyn. She stepped inside the eerie keep, cobwebs and dust everywhere.

Once inside, she yelled again for her brother, hoping her voice would lead Cadyn to her. "Perrin. I'm coming."

Her father struck her head from behind, but she barely flinched. She had purpose now, and she'd not be swayed no matter what the bastard did to her. Two lives depended on her.

Her voice echoed through the empty halls of the keep as she stumbled forward, tripping on loose stones and debris. She heard a faint sound coming from the other end of the hall and quickened her pace, ignoring the pain in her arms from the tight bindings.

Wrath opened a door at the end of the hall and shoved her inside. Once her eyes adjusted to the darkness, she saw Perrin at a table with another lass. They were both tied with rope. "Tryana, ye have come to save me? Where is Cadyn? Brin? Maitland?"

"On their way, I am sure. They will come for us, Perrin. Do not worry." She was so relieved to see the lad was hale. Frightened, but unhurt. And her sister did not look at all like Tryana, but she did look like someone she knew. Ellen was the image of their mother.

Wrath said nothing, instead motioning to another man at the end of the hall to assist him. He pushed her into the chair and said to the guard, "Tie her to the chair." Then he strode toward the end of the hall, calling in two more men from the back door. "Get in here."

She took advantage of his departure to look at her sister. "You are Ellen? Our sister?"

The girl looked timid and petrified. She had brown hair the same color as hers and Perrin's, but she didn't have the same blue eyes as they did. Her eyes were gray, the same as their mother's. Wrath's were brown.

"I think so."

"Where have you lived?"

"Here," she whispered. "With one old woman who cooked for me. I preferred to walk outside.

But now I find out I have a sister and a brother. Why have you not come for me before?"

"Stop talking," Wrath yelled from the back of the hall.

Tryana whispered, "I never knew either of you existed. Ellen, you were born the same day as me but he hid you from our mother. We have an older brother too."

"Is Wulf coming?" Perrin asked.

"Aye. He'll be here before the sun drops. I am certain of it."

"See," Perrin whispered to Ellen. "They will treat ye better than Wrath. I dinnae like him."

Wrath strode back over to them and slapped Perrin. "I said stop talking."

Tryana's fury grew stronger than she'd ever felt before. "Do you feel strong now that you hit a lad, you big bully? How dare you strike him."

"Fine, I'll take it out on you."

Then he hit her with his fist. "Stop talking."

Her head swung to the side, hitting the back of the chair hard enough for her to see stars, so she closed her mouth for a bit. She had to keep her wits and stay alive until Cadyn and Wulf came for them.

Wrath said to the three men who came inside. "One of you over there, and you there, and you there." He sent them to three opposite walls, something that confused her until the three men faced them, each taking out their bow and nocking an arrow.

One asked, "Do you need the others inside?"

"Nay, they can watch for intruders outside. I do expect them eventually. They need to kill them as soon as they see anyone else approach. I do not wish to be bothered inside."

Tryana's belly knotted at his comment, and she couldn't help but wonder if Cadyn were still alive. The bastard planned to kill all of them.

Nay, she had faith in Cadyn's skills and those of his clan. And in her brother Wulf and his wife, Reyna. They'd saved her before, they would do it again.

They just had to stay alive.

Wrath stepped back where he could see all three of their faces, giving them a good view of him. He crossed his arms and said, "Perrin, Tryana is the one who put you in a basket and took you to the nuns. For that she will pay."

None of them spoke, waiting to see what he would say next.

"So, Tryana, this is all up to you. And I will give you a quarter hour to make your decision." He grinned, an evil grin that made the hair stand on the back of her neck. "I could make you decide immediately, but I wish to watch you squirm and struggle first. I don't think the reality of this situation will settle on you unless you are allowed to think on it a bit. I don't want any rash decisions from you."

She had no idea what he was talking about. He spoke like a daft man.

He continued, "I have decided you all don't deserve to live, but I'm leaving the decision up to you." He gave a firm nod to her.

She did not like this reasoning or tone at all. What the hell was he leading to?

"Only one of you will live. Tryana, you will make the decision which one."

Tryana tried to hide the surprise on her face, certain she must have misunderstood him, but she was certain she failed, her breathing and the beat of her heart speeding up so fast that she feared her heart would break out of her chest.

"Who shall I kill, Tryana? It is your choice and your fault. In half the hour, you will give me the name, and one of my men will put an arrow in the middle of their forehead, killing that person instantly."

The three siblings stared at each other, and Tryana feared she would pass out, which could be a blessing. But she did not.

"Your choice, Tryana. Who shall die first?"

CHAPTER TWENTY-THREE

CADYN SAW TWO men coming toward him, two on horseback who looked like they were running in fear. He stopped his horse and grabbed his bow, nocking an arrow. "Halt or I'll put an arrow in yer belly."

The two stopped in front of him, the one nearly in tears. "Please, just let us go. We have no plans to hurt ye. We just wish to get the hell out of here. After what we just heard, we want nothing to do with that daft man."

"I need that information. Ye took a lass, correct? She's the one I'm after. Tell me all ye know about where she is and how many are guarding her and I'll let ye both go."

The second man held his hands up, dropping the reins. "I dinnae care. Dinnae shoot. I'll tell ye all I know."

"Start speaking and I'll let ye know if 'tis enough to save yer hide."

"His name is Wrath. He has a crumbling castle an hour north of here, straight up this path. When ye see the giant oak on each side of the path with arrows in the bark of the tree on the right, take that path. The castle is at the end of that. He had nearly a score men when he hired me. I know not how many he has now, but he's guarding a lad and a lass."

"Guarding. Hell," muttered the first man. "He has a wee laddie tied up like he's a monster. And a timid lass is tied up too. We saw them both before we brought the lass here. The man is daft, but there are too many hired guards there for one man to fight."

Second man said, "And ye cannae pay me enough coin to go back. He's truly daft and evil."

The other man nodded furiously. "He is evil. I can see it in his eyes. Get more men. Ye'll need them. He's hired a keep full of unsavories."

Cadyn grinned. "Now, ye'll do me the honor of telling the next group ye encounter everything ye just told me. The Grant and Ramsay patrol is headed this way."

"No' the Ramsays. I'm going the other way." One man grabbed the reins of the other one.

"Hold on." The man held his hand up to his companion. "We cannot go back that way." He looked to Cadyn. "So if we tell them what we just told ye, they'll no' hurt us? We are only two men."

"And they have a score or more coming, so aye. Be honest, tell them Cadyn said to let ye go. But if ye are lying, I'll come for ye."

"We are no' lying."

"Do as ye are told and ye'll be fine. Now go."

The two took off in a frantic gallop. He was sure Wulf and Reyna would be following him, but he needed to make sure they found the castle. If he were to guess, they'd have split into two groups.

He moved ahead to check the truth of their story. Sure enough, he found the oak trees about a quarter the hour ahead. His mind traveled in four different directions, but this was when his grandsire and his chieftain's teachings came bubbling to the surface, a welcome relief, giving him the focus he needed.

His grandfather's wise words came to him first, "Ye cannae win until ye know how many ye must kill. Scout the area first to find out exactly where the men are hiding. Learn the land first."

Torrian often said, "Ye must find out how many archers are in the trees. They'll kill ye long before the swordsmen will get close enough to fight ye."

That was exactly what he would do. Find a place to leave his horse, then get close enough to count the number of men and whether there were any archers. That was information the group behind him would need for certain.

He left his horse behind a group of bushes and made his way forward. He crept forward, using all the skills he'd been taught over the years—how to travel silently, where to hide, how to cover your tracks, how to use your ears as well as your eyes.

He didn't like what he saw. There were a few archers, but they were busy chatting and laughing. But the number was more than he'd hoped to see. More than a score.

More than two score men were milling about, and while many were not paying attention, some were definitely patrolling the area. If Wrath had that many men, he'd have to wait for more to arrive. He couldn't beat that many on his own.

He needed help. His grandsire would be proud of him. He couldn't head into that group of men without taking an arrow to the chest. He checked behind the towers and to both sides. Men everywhere.

There was one consolation. The two towers looked exactly like the ones in his dream. Now he had to figure out which one Tryana was in. He waited, then noticed the force of men was much heavier around the closest tower.

That's where he would focus his efforts. First, he had to find his help. He found his horse and headed back down the path, following the route he'd taken, knowing the others would be on the same path. He thought of one crossroad he'd passed, so decided perhaps that would be a good place to check.

So he decided to head back to that spot and wait.

As soon as he arrived, he was surprised to find a group of horses coming from the path east of him, instead of the south. They wore plaids he knew, but he waited, grinning when they made it up to him. "Aunt Brigid? Uncle Marcas? I'm glad ye are here." He filled them in on what was transpiring.

Marcas's brother Shaw said, "I'm with ye, Cadyn. Lead the way."

A moment later, the pounding vibrations of horse's hooves came from the northwest. Cadyn turned to see who was approaching, surprised to see the red Grant plaid.

Aunt Brigid said, "More help. Where is Reyna?"

"She's coming, Auntie. Fear no'."

Cadyn waved to Jamie Grant, one of the Grant Chieftains. Connor Grant, his brother with the midnight-colored hair, rode in front with him, at least two score guards behind them. Alasdair, Jake's son, came up alongside his uncles. "We're here to help."

Connor hollered to him, "Where's Dyna, Cadyn? She said to meet us here."

"She sent for ye?"

"Aye, Dobbin came for us. Fastest messenger in all the Highlands." His dark black warhorse with a white mark between its eyes pranced as if ready for battle.

Cadyn heard more horses and pointed. "Here they come." He could see the blue Ramsay plaids in the distance, the two Grant plaids of Alaric's and Dyna's standing out. Reyna and Wulf rode ahead of the others to greet her parents. Once the greetings were done, the three groups joined forces.

Wulf said, "Many thanks to all of ye for helping to put an end to this ridiculous plan of Wrath's. There are three innocent young people involved. I'm giving Dyna and Cadyn lead on this. Cadyn, tell us what ye know."

Cadyn said, "Wrath has both of yer sisters and Perrin tied up in a crumbling castle not far from here with more than two score men. I just came from there and they are surrounding the castle, but most of them are chatting. I didnae see Wrath or yer siblings. I suspect they are in one of the towers. There are some archers, but none posted in trees yet, and the curtain wall is mostly destroyed, not a place to shoot from.

"As ye probably know, he threatened to kill Tryana if anyone followed her, so we must do this carefully. The two men that Wrath hired to transport her were quick to take their payment and run. I stopped them on the path and both men said that Wrath seems daft as well as evil. I don't know what Wrath is usually like, but he seems to be descending into madness."

Connor asked, "Are you certain ye know the way to the castle, Cadyn?"

"Aye, I've checked it on two sides, based on what the two told me before I waited for ye here, even checked the number of guards. I saw Tryana being forced inside the keep. 'Tis true. We just have to decide how to approach without endangering yer siblings, Wulf."

Dyna's gaze carried from one horse to the next. "With all these minds, we'll come up with something."

Cadyn said, "Good. Because when this is over, I wish to ask Tryana to be my wife, with Wulf's permission, of course."

Wulf smiled and nodded. "I can see yer feelings are true."

"They are. Dyna, how shall we do this?"

After a short discussion, the group set off for the castle. It was an unusual group, but he heard Aunt Brigid say, "Reyna, I need yer extra bow."

Cadyn couldn't help but smile. He didn't have his parents or his grandsire here, but he had more help than anyone could ever ask for.

As they approached the castle, Cadyn couldn't help but feel a sense of unease wash over him. The castle stood tall and ominous, with its dark stone walls and two high towers piercing the sky like jagged teeth. Part of the group left their horses behind, cautiously making their way closer, their footsteps muffled by the soft grass underfoot.

As they drew nearer, they noticed movement within the castle walls. Shadows flickered against the stone, and the sound of clanging metal echoed through the air. Cadyn's heart quickened in his chest as he realized that they were not alone.

Worse, there were even more men than he'd anticipated, and many of them were now in the trees.

CHAPTER TWENTY-FOUR

"YOU HAVE SURELY lost your mind. How could you ask me to make such a decision?" Tryana asked. "I've only just met Ellen. I know nothing about her yet they say she is my twin. Is she? Why did you take her away from me? Away from Mama?"

"Because twins bring a curse on a family. I didn't learn of your mother's whoring ways until after you were born. Another child with blue eyes. At least Ellen could be mine. I know who the blue eyes belong to—that carpenter over at Lochluin Abbey. That's why she went to the abbey so often. Not to pray, to be a whore for that man." He paced wildly in front of them, throwing his arm away from his body every so often, as if to emphasize his point.

"I went to chapel with Mama. She always prayed." Tryana had to keep him talking, anything to stall him until Cadyn and the others arrived. She could see he wanted to talk about their mother. "I never saw them together."

"I'm sure she did what she could to hide it from you. Did she leave you in the chapel or the library? Or did she send you outside to garden with the nuns? When I learned of your mother's whoring ways, I locked her in the house, kept her away from that abbey until she gave me a son. I believed Perrin to be my true son, and you took him to the abbey. Now that I see his blue eyes, I know he cannot belong to me. Still, you must pay for your misdeed. It is entirely your fault that I lost my son."

Perrin began to cry. "Please dinnae kill me. Papa, I'll be a good lad. Please dinnae hurt me. And Tryana is a nice lass. She was good to me. I dinnae know Ellen but she looks nice. Please dinnae hurt us. Ye could be my papa. I dinnae have one. I've never had one."

Wrath sent a scathing look at Perrin before he turned away from him. "I'm walking outside to check on my men. When I return, I want your answer, Tryana. Who shall I kill first? Then your next reply will be who I shall kill next. Your choice. You will watch whomever you choose."

Tryana's forehead was covered with sweat, the liquid dripping over her eyebrows and into her eyes. How she prayed Cadyn would be here soon. He had to be or someone would get hurt.

She bowed her head and began to recite prayers, Ellen joining her.

Perrin cried, "Dinnae forget to pray extra for me. I'm no' ten years old yet. Ye willnae pick me, will ye, Tryana? I'm sorry, Ellen, but I will scream. I'm too young."

Tryana said, "I'll not allow him to hurt either of you."

"Ye canno' stop him," Perrin cried, tears in his eyes. "Where's Brin? I need Brin."

"I can prevent him from hurting you. He'll have to kill me first. Since it is my choice, that is what I would choose. Fear not." She wriggled her hands, doing her best to get them free of their bindings. Then she whispered, "Wulf, Cadyn, and Brin will come for us, Perrin, but we must be ready to run. We have to get one of us free."

One of the guards said, "I can hear ye. He'll tie ye up again. Dinnae be foolish. He already hit ye with his fist."

Tryana was quick to respond to the man's foolish warnings. "You are as demented as he is. I hope you do not mind dying either. When the force of Ramsay guards and archers get here, they'll kill all of you."

One of the other guards laughed. "He has a dozen archers in the trees all set to kill anyone who comes near the castle. We are all well trained. We come from the Borderlands, and we don't care about Highlanders."

The door slammed open and Wrath strode back in. "Well, Tryana. Have you made your decision? Who will I kill first?"

All three stayed silent.

"If you do not answer, I'll kill all of you. I can have my men shoot you all at the same time. One arrow for each of you."

"Kill me," she shouted.

Perrin cried, "Nay, Tryana."

"Aye, kill me. If you wish to hurt someone, hurt

me. I am the one you are angry with. Set them free. My choice is me. Kill me and leave them be."

He moved over to stand in front of her, leaning over the table, sneering at her. "Aw, how noble of you. I will gladly kill you. But you were to choose one of them, not yourself. I want you to watch them die. Know that it is all your fault. I've got a fine stick that I plan to set in the fire until it is hot enough to burn your skin. It should help you come up with your answer. But then to kill you? Nay, not yet. You need to watch the two of them suffer, just like you made me suffer."

"You cannot hurt Ellen or Perrin. I'm saying me. I choose me. Kill me."

He moved over to the hearth and set a wooden stick and an iron poker into the flames, heating them both. "But I cannot do that. You see, that would be a failure. I think I'll kill your choice first so you can see me do it. You *must* choose."

He pulled the two weapons out of the flames and walked toward her, getting close enough for her to see the heat, feel it.

"How does it feel?" He briefly touched the end of the stick to her finger.

Tryana screamed.

Screamed and screamed and screamed.

Cadyn and Wulf stood just beyond the point where they would be discovered. Wulf said, "We all go in and save her. 'Tis our only choice."

"Nay," said Cadyn, crossing his arms before he thought, drumming his fingers on his other wrist.

"We need to send a couple of the lasses in first. These men will no' harm a lass without good reason. They will have the chance to get closer, find out how many men are there and where they are located. 'Tis our best chance to scout out the situation while they distract them."

Reyna said, "He is correct. I'll go."

Wulf mumbled, "Why must it always be ye, Reyna?"

She winked at him and grinned. "Because I know exactly what to do."

Dyna jumped in, "And I'll go along too. The two of us can handle a few surly men."

Wulf hadn't wanted to agree to their plan, but he knew the argument was sound, so he finally went along. One sound from Reyna and he'd be at her side, everyone knew that. And so would her father. So the rest hid in the forest, some in the trees while the two made their first approach.

Reyna and Dyna rode up to the castle wall on their horses, looking around the area as if they'd never been there before.

Reyna said, "We are surely lost. Ross land is closer to Inverness, I think."

"We are a long way from Inverness. We've only been traveling for less than an hour." Dyna noticed a man near the open gates. "Could ye help us, please? We are trying to travel to our uncle's place, but we are lost. I thought we were to go near an oak tree and that would take us straight to the firth. Once we saw water, then we were to head north. Are ye near water?"

The man said, "Move on. I am no' yer guide."

Dyna said, "But I'm sure we are in the right place." Then the two began to argue, just as Cadyn had suggested because it would confuse the guards.

Reyna barked out, "Nay, ye are the fool, Fiona. I told ye we were going the wrong way."

"Ye are the fool, Hilda. Ye always think ye are smarter than me just because ye know the men want ye so."

"I canno' help it if men prefer my looks." Reyna thrust her chest out. "What say ye, soldier?"

"I say move along." His eyes didn't agree with his words, his eyes drawn to Reyna's chest.

"I'll allow ye to touch them if ye tell us which way to go." Reyna smiled and winked at him.

"Be quiet, Hilda. We dinnae have time for this."

Three men dropped out of the trees. "I'll tell ye if ye let me touch them."

"Nay, me first."

One shoved the other. "I said it first so I get first touch."

Before they knew it, there were ten men arguing over Reyna. It was exactly what they needed. Cadyn had said few men would kill a lass on site without asking questions, and he'd been correct. While they brought all the attention to themselves, the others were checking the trees for archers, some went around back, some climbed the castle wall on the side. And Cadyn saw several climb into the trees the men were hopping out of, simply because they wished to look closely at Reyna.

Cadyn climbed onto the crumbling curtain

wall from a tree he'd been in, his gaze locked on the activity in the front while he tossed a rope down to Wulf. "Easy climb while yer wife has them all entranced."

"I canno' watch or I'll put my fist in a few faces." Wulf's jaw was as tense as he'd ever seen it, and he understood so he said nothing.

"We have a plan, so forget those fools and what they are doing." Cadyn reminded him, "We go inside and I'll do the bird call to pull Reyna and Dyna forward while the others already in place take those men out of commission. We need the four of us inside. We'll save them, dinnae worry. Ye will draw his attention enough so I can sneak around back, get him from behind."

Wulf stared up at a hawk flying overhead. "I pray we do. I have a sister I adore inside, plus two new siblings I must get to know. I should have killed him the first time."

Then something happened that changed everything—Tryana screamed. And the first arrow flew.

Wulf raced over to the tower door, opened it, and yelled, "Let her go, Wrath, ye rotten bastard. Have ye nae conscience at all?" Reyna and Dyna came in directly behind Wulf while Cadyn moved around to the back entrance. Arrows sluiced through the air in the courtyard, the painful yells from the men letting them know they found their targets.

Reyna said, "Dinnae worry, Tryana. We are here."

Perrin cried out, "Will ye save me too, Wulf? Please?"

"Aye, I am here for my brother. I'll not let ye be hurt."

Wrath grabbed Tryana by the hair and yanked her out of the chair, tilting her head back so he could hold the hot poker not far from her neck while he hid behind her. "Leave us or I'll blind her right now."

Perrin cried while Dyna and Reyna moved to either side of Wulf. Cadyn found his way easily in the back entrance and snuck inside where he could see the three assessing the area. He was nearly behind Wrath when the man said to his archers. "Kill the women, will you please, so I can deal with my son without interruption?"

Reyna and Dyna were faster, killing two archers while Wulf unsheathed his sword and cut down the man behind him with one swing. "I should never have let ye live before, Wrath," Wulf grumbled. "Now 'tis just ye and me, ye old bastard. Ye've left enough cruelty on this land. Time to end it."

"And how are you going to strike me down from there? Tryana will be dead before you ever get here. You think you are better than me? You are a fool."

"Nay, I am no', but I know someone who is better than ye. Reyna?"

Wrath de Gray laughed. "You think a woman can hurt me? She's as ignorant as your sister. What a fool you are to believe a woman has any value."

Cadyn knew what was coming. Reyna fired her

arrow, catching Wrath in the neck, just missing his artery. Cadyn leaped from behind him and pulled Tryana to the side, far enough away from him so his hot poker would not touch her reflexively.

"Nice shot, Reyna," Dyna whooped, then whistled loud enough for everyone to hear.

The man crumpled to the ground, clutching at the arrow. Reyna strode over and gazed down at him, placing her boot on his belly. "I could have hit ye between the eyes, but this is more rewarding. But do ye know why?" She glanced over her shoulder and Wulf came behind her, wrapping his arm around her, kissing her cheek.

"That was a perfect shot. You're a fierce protector, my love."

Dyna stood next to her, and the expression in Wrath's eyes was the look of total disgust. "Why not between the eyes, Reyna? 'Tis yer best shot."

"This was advice from Auntie Brenna. I put it in his neck because he'll pull on it and then slice the big vessel open. Basically finishing it himself. Perfect for someone who is as cruel as he has been his whole life."

The man's eyes locked on Wulf. "Help....me."

Wulf smiled. "I think no' after all the pain ye've caused me and my siblings. Good riddance to ye, and the irony of it is ye will do it to yerself."

Just as Brenna had said he would, he pulled the arrow out of his neck, his blood shooting across the floor. The life left his eyes in less than a moment.

The hall filled with warriors in a matter of seconds. Brin reached Perrin quickly, untying him just in time for the boy to throw himself into Brin's arms, sobbing.

Wulf found his way to Ellen, untying her. "I'm yer eldest brother, Ellen. My name is Wulfstan. So pleased to make yer acquaintance. I hope we have many years together as a family."

Tryana's arms were in a tight grip around Cadyn's neck. She sobbed onto his shoulder while he undid all her ties, protecting her finger as best he could. "I have ye, lass. Did ye think for a moment I wouldnae come for ye?"

The door banged, a sound he recognized, his grandsire's signature. Surprised to see him, he lifted Tryana into his arms and set her down next to her sister. "Ellen, I hope ye get to know yer dear sister someday soon. I love her with all my heart."

Tryana sobbed and wrapped her arms around her sister.

"What about me?" Perrin stood in front of her.

Tryana stepped back to look at her younger brother. "I'll never forget ye, Magni," she said giggling with happiness as she hugged him.

Then he wriggled away from her and said, "This is the best day ever. Look at all these warriors who came for us, Tryana. And I have a brother and two sisters!"

Tryana said, "Will ye promise not to run away this time, Perrin? Please give us a chance. I think you will love Ramsay land."

He said, "Can I sleep with the warriors?"

"You can sleep wherever ye like," she replied as he raced over to Brin.

Cadyn's grandfather and father made their way through the crowd, Grandda finally stopping in front of Wrath and whistled. "I'd recognize that hit anywhere. Reyna, ye are just like my Gwynie." His hands went to his hips, then turned to Cadyn. "Ye did exactly what I told ye no' to do, lad."

Cadyn nodded as he reached for Tryana's hand, tucking her next to him and kissing her forehead. "I did and I have no regrets. Meet my future wife, if I am lucky enough to have her agree to marry me."

She squealed, "Aye!" hugging Cadyn and planting a big kiss on his lips before she turned away blushing, her gaze dropping to her feet.

"Ye've chosen well, Cadyn. Welcome to the family, Tryana." His father clasped his shoulder, then said, "I'm going back out to find Ceit."

Grandda came over to stand in front of him. "I was hoping ye would do just as ye did. Nice job, Grandson. Ye make this old man proud."

Cadyn couldn't hide his shock. "Ye wished I would run off on my own? But ye told me *no'* to."

"Aye, 'tis how it works with stubborn young lads. Ye tell him one thing, and they'll do the opposite." Then he bussed Tryana's cheek. "Welcome to the clan, lass."

Cadyn was speechless.

CHAPTER TWENTY-FIVE

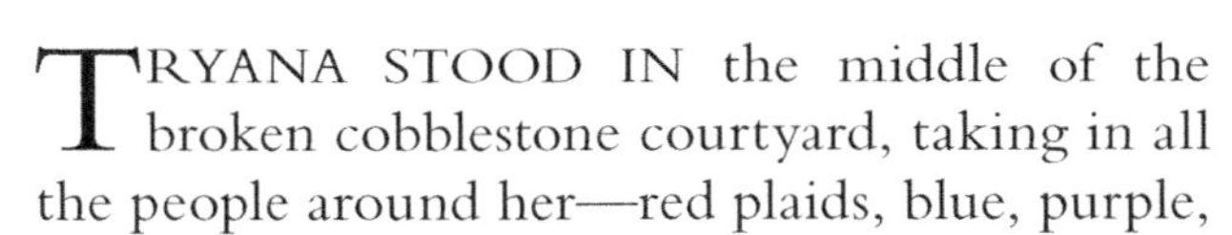

TRYANA STOOD IN the middle of the broken cobblestone courtyard, taking in all the people around her—red plaids, blue, purple, gold, so many glorious colors. It was the middle of the night and they had nowhere to go.

A loud whistle caught their attention. The two Highlanders in red plaids held their hands up and said, "'Tis too late to go elsewhere. Grant land is half the hour from here. Ye are all invited for a short feast before we fall into our beds to sleep. Any warrior knows that 'tis too soon to sleep after battle."

Perrin ran over in front of Connor and asked, "May I come along, please? I've never been to Grant land."

Connor reached down and lifted the lad up and set him on his horse. "Ye can lead the way, lad." Then he mounted behind him.

Perrin laughed so hard that Tryana was enraptured, watching the lad. Cadyn had left to gather the horses for everyone. She could have watched Perrin forever but then she looked at her sister standing next to her. "You look lost, Ellen."

Ellen smiled weakly. "I think my life is about to change for the better, but I've never been around so many people before. Will you help me learn how to act the way I should? Will you sleep in the same chamber with me? Explain everything to me? I know it will take a while, but I wish to get to know my siblings. Get to know everyone. You all worked together so well."

She took her sister's hand and said, "I will help you. We had a cruel father, but I look forward to telling you all about our dear mother, God rest her soul. You look exactly like her."

Dyna motioned them all out the gates, so she held Ellen's hand as she peered about for Cadyn and the horses. "Can you ride a horse?"

She shook her head. "I wish to learn, but I've never been away from this old castle. The old woman who took care of me left as soon as Wrath came along. He sent her away and told me he was my father. He is not?"

"Nay. It's a long story I'll tell you in our chamber when we are alone. I'll find someone you can ride with."

She stepped into the group and found Cadyn coming toward them. "Cadyn, she cannot ride on her own."

Alaric was next to him and said, "She can ride with me." He dismounted and helped her onto the horse. He could see how nervous she was. "Ye've never ridden?"

"Nay, I was kept hidden away." Her gaze fell.

"Dinnae worry, lass. I'll no' let ye fall and this is a celebratory ride back to Grant Castle. This is the most fun ye will have ever had." Alaric mounted behind her, taking his extra plaid and wrapping it around her since it was chilly, then he wrapped it around his back. "This will keep ye from falling."

Ellen gave Tryana a wee smile and waved.

Cadyn helped Tryana up and mounted behind her. As a group, they took off toward Grant land, a number of guards staying behind to bury the dead and take the others to the magistrate. He kissed her neck and said, "I'll ask ye again on the morrow. I dinnae wish to think ye were pressured into saying aye to my proposal."

She turned to look at him from the side. "Cadyn, I'll never change my mind. You are the only one for me."

The Grant war whoop came from behind them so he set his horse to a gallop and let out the Ramsay war whoop, others joining him, while Tryana covered her ears, laughing and looking over at Ellen. Her new sister tipped her head back and laughed heartily, bouncing on the horse as Alaric let out his Grant whoop.

They weren't gone long before they arrived on Grant land. Tryana took one look at the beautiful castle sitting up on a small hill, looking so majestic with the many torches on the curtain wall lighting up the area. "Oh my. I've never seen a castle like this. Have you been here before, Cadyn?"

"Many times. I'll take us to the inside stable, let the guards stop out here." He followed Alaric inside the castle wall. "Wait until ye see the inside.

Alex and Maddie Grant made a beautiful castle, adding towers and extra floors, though they have both passed on. Each of their children lives in their own tower, except Connor's family who lives on the third floor. The second floor is for guests. They have a beautiful lake for our festivals, and Uncle Alex even made Aunt Maddie and his daughters a special bathing chamber inside. Ye'll see it on the morrow."

Wulf and Reyna waited for them, and Perrin joined them once he hopped off Connor's horse with his own imitation of a Grant war whoop. "That was the most fun I've ever had, Connor. Tryana, did ye see how fast we were galloping?"

When she dismounted, she said to Cadyn, "I think I need to join my siblings, help make my sister comfortable. Do you mind?"

"Nay, ye should. I'll move about a bit to talk to others, but I'll return." He kissed her cheek and escorted her inside, leading her to the great hall, already with two hearths ablaze and warming the inside. He settled her and Ellen at a seat by the closest hearth, gave them each a fur for their laps, then left to find them a beverage.

Reyna sat next to Ellen while Wulf stood leaning against the stone next to the hearth. "Ye are about to taste some wonderful food, Ellen. The Grant cook is almost as good as the Ramsay cook. The fruit tarts are delicious, especially the berry ones."

Ellen glanced over at Tryana and smiled. "I've never had a berry tart. What are they?"

Perrin overheard and said, "I'll find ye one and

two for me." He took off to a trestle table that was being covered with food—breads, cheeses, meat pies, chicken legs. And fruit tarts. All different kinds. He picked out three and brought them over. "Which one would ye like, Ellen?"

"You choose for me."

Perrin gave her the berry tart, gave a cherry tart to Tryana, and asked, "Would ye like this one, Reyna? I can get another."

"Nay, ye eat that one."

The three ate their sweets, and Ellen's wide-eyes told them everything. "These are heavenly," she whispered, taking another bite of the juicy treat. "Do you know everyone here?" she asked Tryana.

"Nay, but Reyna does."

Wulf said, "Please help us, Reyna. Even I dinnae know half of the people here. I need to learn before ye introduce us."

Ellen said, "Tell me some of the groupings so I understand more of what everyone discusses. The different clans and so on." She turned her chair sideways as Reyna and Tryana did the same.

Reyna explained, "The far group is the Ramsay group. Grandda Logan and Uncle Cailean are speaking with my mother and father. My da is the chieftain of Clan Matheson. I'll go see them in a wee bit. Brin Cameron," she pointed to a man Perrin had run over to speak with. "He lives in a small castle near Lochluin Abbey, close by where Tryana and Wulf grew up. He is speaking with Ceit, Cadyn's sister, and he seems quite interested in her." Reyna waggled her brow at Wulf. "Have ye noticed, Wulf?"

"I have. They make a fine couple, I think."

Reyna continued, "And that group is the two Grant chieftains, Connor and Jamie, with Connor's daughter Dyna and her husband, Derric. The dark-haired woman is their sister, Kyla, and the blonde is Jamie's wife, Gracie. They are the parents of Alaric, the man ye rode with, Ellen. There are many others, but those are the groups for now. Camerons, Grants, Ramsays, and Mathesons. It all began when Alex Grant's sister Brenna married Quade Ramsay, Logan's brother. But for now, I think Wulf and I should talk with my parents. We'll talk again on the morrow, Ellen."

Reyna and Wulf left and Ellen turned to Tryana. "I have much to learn, but I'm verra pleased to have a sister. But I have a question for you. Where will we live? May I live with you? I have nowhere to go."

"Aye. We will live together. We'll chat with Wulf on the morrow. But I think we should find a hut of our own near Ramsay land. I hope to marry Cadyn someday soon, but I need to get to know my new family first. After all that has happened, and you'll learn eventually, I wish to belong to a clan who can protect us. So it should be Clan Ramsay or Clan Cameron."

Ellen turned back to the crowd as tears streamed down her face.

Tryana whispered, "What's wrong?"

"Naught. Everything is right. I'm so happy to have you and Perrin and Wulf. But I also hope to have friends."

Tryana squeezed her hand.

"I've never had a friend before."

Tryana replied, "Neither have I."

CHAPTER TWENTY-SIX

One moon later, Ramsay land

CADYN AND WULF stood outside the cottage they were building inside the curtain wall of Castle Ramsay discussing the interior. The cottage was nearly ready to be thatched, but first they had to decide where the interior walls would be going. The outside was completed, and the cottage was large.

Cadyn's father joined them. "Evening, Cailean," Wulf said. "We are doing our best to decide how many bedchambers we need to have."

Cadyn's Grandda joined them next. "Just make it two chambers. One for living and one for sleeping."

Before they knew it, Gavin joined them also. He started with the questions. "How many will be living here?"

Cadyn explained, "Wulf and Reyna have their own bedchamber, and once Tryana and I are wed, we will have our own bedchamber. We need a third bedchamber for Ellen and Perri."

Gavin said, "So three bedchambers and one

living chamber. 'Tis easy enough to figure out. Divide the end into three chambers and the rest is living space."

Wulf said, "Not quite. Reyna and I will have bairns so we want a larger chamber. The cottage is plenty big enough to put two bedchambers on each end. Living chamber in the middle."

Reyna joined them. "Nay, one small chamber on the far end will be the garderobe so I willnae have to go outside."

Cadyn sighed because he knew exactly what was about to happen. His father and grandfather were about to start an argument about which was the better plan, then Gavin would agree with Grandda. Others would join them just to be part of the argument. It seemed to be a Ramsay tradition.

Sure enough, Grandda said, "Three on the end. Dinnae act like a spoiled lass, Reyna. Ye dinnae need a special bedchamber. The stone walls will be too thick and use up too much space."

Reyna crossed her arms and argued, "I am no' spoiled, Grandda. Please mind yer tongue. Da said he would build walls of timber inside my home. 'Twill give us privacy and more room. This is no' a castle and no' a peasant's home."

Wulf confirmed, "Marcas said he would. Said they are easy to build and do well inside the stone walls."

His father said, "Ye should have built separate cottages. Why build such a large one? 'Tis wasteful to me."

Gavin added, "Ye could have built three. Build

another one outside the curtain wall. We have plenty of room out there. We can build ye a manor home."

Before he knew it, they were all arguing. Various comments came to him.

"Why be difficult?"

"'Twill take forever."

"Two chambers in a home are enough."

"Ye must have a large hearth at the end, no' in the middle."

"Ye dinnae need to cook, just heat the place."

"Ye can eat at the keep."

"I'm building two chambers."

"I'm building three chambers."

"I'll start with four chambers."

Cadyn listened to the group for a wee bit, but then decided they would never agree on anything. He let out a shrill whistle and yelled, "Silence!"

Grandda turned around and snarled, "Dinnae tell me to be quiet, lad. Ye will regret it."

Wulf, Reyna, Gavin, Da, Grandda, and now Marcas and Perrin all stared at him, waiting to hear what he had to say.

"This home is to belong to Wulf and Reyna, and Tryana and me. Once the three weddings take place, we need to have this finished so we will proceed as we agreed to build it. We decided to have the living space in the center and four chambers, two on either end. Marcas has said he will teach us how to use timber for the walls instead of just the beams. We are pleased with this idea so we will go ahead with it."

Grandda asked, "Why must ye do everything

differently? Ye could have built a manor home outside the wall. Ye could..."

"Grandda! Stop!" He held his hand up because he had to put an end to this constant interference. "We chose inside the walls because Tryana, Ellen, and Perrin feel safer inside the walls. And with all that was thrust upon them, Wulf and I felt it a reasonable request. It's being built here and with four bedchambers. Done."

"Cadyn, ye always disagree with me. Why? Do ye no' appreciate my help?" Grandda asked.

Gavin said, "Da, dinnae be ridiculous. Cadyn has tried to be just like ye ever since he was born. He walks like ye, talks like ye, shoots like ye, he even follows ye."

"Aye," Cailean said. "Even I've seen it. 'Tis the ultimate compliment when someone tries to be like ye."

Cadyn growled, "Och, have any of ye ever thought that I dinnae do it apurpose? That I truly walk like him? That I truly have the same voice as he does? I dinnae think about the way I walk. I just walk and it comes out like Grandda. Stop telling me I imitate him. I dinnae."

His grandfather arched a brow at him. "I'm sorry ye feel that way, Cadyn. I thought ye loved me."

He sighed. "Of course I love and admire ye. But I am my own man."

"Seems ye are." The old beast narrowed his gaze at him, then walked away.

His father smiled and clasped his shoulder. "Ye are a fine man, and Mama and I are verra proud of ye. Ye chose a fine wife, and ye will make a good father to yer bairns. Ignore Grandda. Some get fussy as they age."

"I'm no' fussy." The shout came from the front of the keep just before the door slammed shut. Louder than usual, if that were possible. Some lost their hearing as they aged, but not his grandfather.

His hands settled on his hips. "Many thanks, Da." Then he raised his voice. "I love ye too, Grandda."

"He loves ye, Cadyn."

"I know he does, in his own, odd way. I thought after all we've gone through, the patrol, the baron, Wulf's sire, that Grandda would be proud of me. I dinnae know what it takes."

A few days later, Tryana was surprised to awaken to a warm and beautiful day with the autumn season around the corner. She still slept in the Ramsay keep in the same chamber as Ellen. Perrin had slept with them for a while, but now he preferred to sleep with the guards in the stable. Though she'd noticed that on the nights when the lightning came streaking across the sky, he found his way onto the floor on a stack of pillows in their chamber.

But today was a lovely day. She and Ellen had just finished breaking their fast when Cadyn came inside. "Good morn to ye both, ladies." He leaned down and gave Tryana a kiss. "Hmmm, I taste honey on yer oats."

She blushed and nodded.

"Tryana, could I invite ye for a ride across the meadow? 'Tis a beautiful day. Would ye mind, Ellen?"

Tryana looked at her sister who'd become so dear to her in such a short time. "Do ye mind?"

"Nay, I'd promised to help Lady Brenna this morn in her healing chamber. We're going to clean it and cut more linen strips. She likes to keep her cupboards well stocked. Go and enjoy yourself, sister." She left for the end of the hall, her steps brisk as though she were excited to join Brenna. Ellen enjoyed learning the skill of healing.

Cadyn held his hand out. "I dinnae think ye will need yer mantle, though I have a couple of extra plaids if the weather turns. I thought I would take ye for a ride to our loch. Mayhap go for a quick swim?"

"But I cannot swim," she whispered, her shoulders sagging.

"Then I will teach ye. 'Tis no' so hard."

She took his hand and they walked out of the keep and out of the gates to where his horse stood waiting.

"He looks ready to go," she said, patting his withers.

"He loves to gallop across the meadow."

Off they headed toward the loch. The day was indeed lovely and she tipped her head back to take in the sun. "It is so warm today, unusually warm, do you not think so, Cadyn?"

"I do," he said, his hand tucking her tight against him.

Once they arrived, she had a sudden question. "Cadyn, what will I wear in the water? Perrin swam with nothing on." He helped her dismount, then led her to the water's edge, taking in the beauty of the sun reflecting on the loch.

He grinned at her. "'Tis what I usually wear. Naught. We will be husband and wife soon, but I can duck in quickly while yer head is turned."

He waited for her answer, but she didn't have one ready. "Cadyn, may I ask you another question?"

"Aye, I'll answer if I can." He moved closer, taking her hand in his. "This is difficult for ye?"

"Aye." She lifted her gaze to his and said the most honest words that had settled in her heart two days ago. "Could we handfast and not wait for the wedding? I've overheard Isla and Reyna speak of their lovemaking and I don't wish to wait. They explained it all to me, but I would prefer to know about it now."

"Truly?"

"You look stunned. We do not have to if you wish to wait."

He stepped closer, cupped her face, and settled his lips on hers. It was a soft kiss, something she enjoyed more than she would ever admit to anyone. Parting her lips, she touched her tongue to his and he groaned, tugging her closer until their bodies felt as one but for the fabric between them. She didn't want that fabric there any longer.

Their tongues mated and he angled his mouth over hers, deepening the kiss. Her breasts tingled in response and she had the sudden urge to remove all her clothing.

Cadyn ended the kiss as if he sensed her need growing. He took her hand and took a strip of his plaid, wrapping it over their intertwined fingers. He gazed into her eyes and said, "Tryana de Gray, I pledge myself to ye. I pledge to love and protect ye for as long as ye wish me to do so. We could break our pledge since it's a handfasting, but I pledge to ye that I will never break this pledge."

Her heart swelled and she stared at their hands, then back at his handsome face. Locking gazes with him, she said, "I did not know it was possible to love anyone the way I love you, Cadyn MacAdam. I pledge my love to you, and I pledge it will never waver. I wish to love you and share everything with you for the rest of our lives."

He kissed her lightly on the lips, then on the cheek. He took her hand and returned to his horse, taking out another plaid and leading her over to the base of a tree covered with soft grass and moss. It was a perfect spot because if anyone came, they would never be seen.

He arranged the plaid on the ground and then helped her to get comfortable. She removed her gown but left her chemise on, her dignity not ready to remove it yet.

"Lass, ye are the most beautiful woman I've ever seen. Ye need not be shy with me, but 'tis our first time, so I understand."

Then Cadyn spent a long time teaching her how wonderful true love could be.

She learned how it felt to be caressed, treasured,

adored. Feelings she'd never thought possible. How lips felt on her skin, on her neck, her shoulders, her breasts.

Even her nipples. And how she enjoyed the touch, the caress, the joining of the two as one. She learned about his strong body and learned even more about her own. This was a way she could please him privately, something she loved. Cadyn worried so about her pain, but she did not care because she considered it a lovely part of their consummation.

She'd had no idea that love between a man and a woman could be so wonderful, so pleasurable. So passionate. That she could give herself to this man so fully, and he would do the same to her. That it was an amazing experience of intimacy, of exploring each other, of giving to the other strictly to heighten one's pleasure.

She would indeed love this man until her last breath.

And after he taught her how to truly love another, he taught her how to swim. Before they left, he gave her a package, something that told her how thoughtful he was—the two Bibles she thought were lost forever. Her mother's and the one given to her by the abbess.

Her life couldn't possibly get any better than this day they'd shared.

EPILOGUE

Mid-Autumn, Ramsay land

TRYANA STOOD INSIDE the Ramsay great hall, dressed in her finery and ready to go to her wedding.

This day would prove to be very special. She would say her vows to become Cadyn's wife, Wulf was marrying Reyna, and Isla was marrying Grif. All three of them together on Ramsay land.

It had been a wonderful few weeks as they'd planned the ceremony and built a place to live, and she'd learned more and more about her beloved Cadyn MacAdam. He and Wulf had built a brand new cottage in the farthest corner inside the curtain wall, one with four bedchambers and a garderobe. Tryana was excited about moving into their new home, moving out of the bedchamber abovestairs to the cottage they would share with Reyna and Wulf. Cadyn had gone back to his chamber in the main castle, but after the wedding they'd move into their own chamber in the cottage.

Isla and Grif would be returning to Matheson

land while Wulf and Reyna agreed to split their time between Ramsay land and Black Isle.

How she'd enjoyed making new friends and getting to know all her siblings. She'd learned to use a bow, how to sew leggings, and spent much of her time teaching Ellen and Perrin how to read and write. The lad had started learning his letters with the nuns, but he had improved greatly, helping Ellen as they progressed.

She was happy and found her work fulfilling. She and Ellen had helped with her wedding dress too, though they'd carefully planned the three dresses to coordinate with each other since they would be marrying on the same day. Though their dresses were all a different color, the ribbons in the bodice were the same shade of lavender.

Tryana's dress was a pale blue, Reyna's a lovely yellow, and Isla's was a light green. As the three lasses stood side by side, adorned in their beautiful dresses, Tryana couldn't help but feel a sense of pride. She had worked tirelessly to ensure that every stitch of fabric, every bead and ribbon was perfect. And now, seeing her friends in their dresses, Tryana knew that her hard work had paid off. The lavender ribbons complemented each of the dresses, and Tryana especially loved the beading at the neckline of her blue gown.

She proudly wore the pearl necklace that was the one thing she still had of her mother's.

To her surprise, Perrin had come to her last eve with a surprise. He'd held his hand out to her and said, "I wish for ye to have this." He handed her a small package wrapped in twine. She thought she'd seen something similar fall from his clothing near the waterfall when he'd gotten upset that she'd touched his clothes.

"What is it, Perrin?"

"'Tis something the abbess gave me a long time ago. She said my sire made it for my mother, but since they had both passed on, the abbess thought I should have it. But I wish for ye to have it for yer wedding on the morrow. I peeked at it but 'tis no' for me."

She'd opened it through teary eyes, surprised to see a beautiful pearl brooch inside, the pearl nestled in the center of a small carved wooden rose. "Oh, Perrin. This is lovely."

"I dinnae wish to wear it because I am a Highlander now."

"There is something else inside. A piece of parchment. Have you looked at it, Perrin?"

"Nay, I peeked once, but when I saw it was a piece of jewelry, I didnae look any further. 'Tis for a lass."

She unfolded the parchment, surprised to see writing on the paper.

Dear Perrin, Wulf, and Tryana,

I write this as an apology, for not being able to be in your lives. My mother was English so Glenna's parents would not allow our marriage to go through, especially since I am not of noble blood. But we handfasted because I loved your mother with all my heart, but now she is gone. I wish I could raise you, but Wrath would never allow it. I tried to speak with Wrath long ago to end the marriage so I could be a good father to you, but he took his anger out on my dear Glenna, your mother. I feared he would kill her.

I send this to let you know that your mother had the most beautiful heart of anyone I know and we both adored all of you. May God bless you all forever.

Morris Brown

Underneath the note sat a small dagger with a note attached to it. "For Perrin."

Perrin's face lit up and he took it in his hand, admiring it. "He didnae forget me."

She smiled and said, "Many thanks to you. I would love to wear the brooch on the morrow. And I'll share it with our sister. She can wear it when she marries." She hugged him close, but he wriggled out of her arms. "And I'll save the note so our brother can read it also."

"I have to go see Wulf." Then he'd disappeared. How her life had changed ever since Wulf had stolen her away from the baron. And it had changed in the most wonderful ways.

As they made their way toward the chapel, Tryana's heart began to race. She had known she was in love with Cadyn from the moment they had met. Even in the abbey north of York, ironically named Ellonton Abbey, Cadyn's steel gaze had a way of setting her insides to fluttering. And now, as she walked towards him, she could feel her heart pounding in her chest.

Cadyn MacAdam was the only one for her. Just looking at his golden hair, his green eyes, and the wide smile he always had for her set her belly into a flurry of butterflies. How blessed she was that Cadyn loved her. Only her. How had she become so fortunate?

As she reached the altar, Cadyn turned towards her, his eyes sparkling with love and admiration. Tryana felt her cheeks flush as he took her hand in his.

The ceremony passed in a blur of joy and happiness. Ramsay land was a sea of different plaids—Ramsay and Matheson the most predominant. As the newlywed couples made their way back down the aisle, Tryana felt her heart overflow with love for her new husband. They headed to the courtyard to greet many of the clan, then would head into the great hall for the evening feast and festival.

The clan would feed the entire Ramsay clan and any neighbors, but the family would be inside the hall. There were so many Grants, Camerons, Mathesons, Menzies, and Drummonds here that she swore she'd never learn all their names.

But until then, they would greet the people of the Ramsay village who worked so hard for the clan. This was the only time they were to be available for anyone who wished to greet them.

The three couples moved into the center of the courtyard, surrounded by a group of Ramsay guards along with the well-wishers. Suddenly exhausted, Tryana leaned her head onto her husband's shoulder and sighed. She'd made it through the ceremony and they were now husband and wife. The rest did not truly matter.

Then the tension in her husband's body changed.

"What is it, Cadyn?" she whispered, taking in the clench of his jaw that he did his best to hide along with the involuntary flex of his fists.

"I dinnae know, but I will take care of it, love," he said, giving her a quick kiss on the lips before he turned away.

Tryana watched as her husband weaved his way through the crowd, his broad shoulders brushing past people as he moved. She knew he was searching for the source of his unease, and she couldn't help but feel a sense of pride in him. Cadyn was a fierce protector, and she knew that he would do anything to ensure her safety.

As she waited for Cadyn to return, Tryana noticed a figure lurking in the shadows. It was a man, dressed head to toe in black, with a hood pulled low over his face. Tryana's heart raced as she realized that this man was not one of the wedding guests. Was he a villager? Fear clawed at her insides. Her sire was dead, but the baron had survived. He'd been taken to the magistrate, but was it possible he had been released, able to attack her or steal her away yet again?

She glanced around, but no one else seemed to have noticed the intruder. Without thinking, Tryana stepped forward, putting herself between the man and her friends and family.

"Who are you?" she demanded, trying to keep her voice steady despite the fear that was rising in her chest.

The man said nothing, but he stepped forward, his hand reaching out to grab her. Tryana instinctively stepped back, her hand reaching for the dagger she kept hidden in her dress.

"I'm your husband, not that fool." He whispered the words so the others wouldn't overhear his threat. Even with the hood on, she knew, without a doubt, that this man was the baron. Still disgruntled over losing her.

The man lunged forward, and Tryana pulled out her dagger just in time, slashing at his arm. The man let out a cry of pain, but he didn't stop. Instead, he charged forward, his hands reaching for her, a blade of his own appearing in his hand.

Tryana held her ground, her dagger poised and ready. Cadyn had made good on his promise to show her how to use a dagger, but of course she had never used one in a fight before. But she wouldn't let this man harm her or her loved ones. As he closed in on her, she swung her dagger again, this time aiming for his chest.

But she never touched him. He stopped just out of reach of her dagger with a look of shock on his face that surprised her.

Everyone else seemed to notice all at once, screams rending the air. Shouts of "kill him" and "stop him" echoed through the courtyard. But no one else needed to move.

The baron stumbled back, clutching his side, blood now covering his hands. He looked at the dark fluid in his hands, then back at her. "But you are *my* wife." He tried to say something else, but an odd sound came from his throat along with a mouth full of bloody spittle. He fell forward, landing on his face, clutching his side. As he fell, Cadyn yanked his weapon out of the man's flank.

"The bastard would not give up," he said, as if he needed an explanation to kill the man who had kidnapped and beat her on multiple occasions. "How many times is he allowed to attack ye?" He reached for her and asked, "Are you all right, love?"

Cailean MacAdam came up from behind him, clasped his shoulder and said, "Give me that weapon. I'll clean it, Cadyn."

Then Logan pushed Cailean aside and said, "Nay. Allow me. The lad is nearly as smart as I am so I'll clean his sword."

Tryana glanced at her husband, his eyes wide in shock at his grandfather's statement. "My thanks, Grandda."

His grandfather stood close to him after cleaning the weapon and returning it. He said, "Ye warm this old man's insides because ye fight like me, and ye look a wee bit like me."

His grandmother came up behind his grandfather and said, "Logan, he is ye. He walks like ye, talks like ye, and thinks like ye."

"If Gwynie believes it, it must be so." Logan's eyes teared up, but then he nearly jumped on his grandson and gave him the biggest hug he'd ever given anyone. "Ye make this old man verra proud, Cadyn."

Cadyn looked at his wife and said, "Ye are my good luck charm, Tryana. I never thought I'd see the day he hugged me."

Logan pushed away from him and then winked. "Ye better remember it well. Ye'll no' get another."

THE END

www.keiramontclair.com

DEAR READER,

Thank you for reading Cadyn and Tryana's story. No "cliff hanger" this time.

By the way, I never considered the other two novels to have cliff hanger endings, only teasers. But so many of you called them cliff hangers that I decided not to do one for this book.

No teasers—no cliff hanger! I know the one about the evil Wulf capturing Reyna would be a big teaser, so I get it!

Next up will be Ceit and Brin's story, but you won't see it until September. I have much planned for the summer, so I plan to relax a bit.

Then for Christmas, you'll see Maitland and Maeve's story, the one that came to me when I had a muddled Covid brain. That will be book 5 in this ongoing series.

Enjoy your summer!

Happy reading,

Keira Montclair

NOVELS BY
KEIRA MONTCLAIR

HIGHLAND HUNTERS

THE SCOT'S CONFLICT
THE SCOT'S TRAITOR
THE SCOT'S PROTECTOR

HIGHLAND HEALERS

THE CURSE OF BLACK ISLE
THE WITCH OF BLACK ISLE
THE SCOURGE OF BLACK ISLE
THE GHOSTS OF BLACK ISLE
THE GIFT OF BLACK ISLE

THE CLAN GRANT SERIES

#1- RESCUED BY A HIGHLANDER-
Alex and Maddie
#2- HEALING A HIGHLANDER'S HEART-
Brenna and Quade
#3- LOVE LETTERS FROM LARGS-
Brodie and Celestina
#4-JOURNEY TO THE HIGHLANDS-
Robbie and Caralyn
#5-HIGHLAND SPARKS-
Logan and Gwyneth
#6-MY DESPERATE HIGHLANDER-
Micheil and Diana

#7-THE BRIGHTEST STAR IN THE HIGHLANDS-
Jennie and Aedan
#8- HIGHLAND HARMONY-
Avelina and Drew
#9-YULETIDE ANGELS

THE HIGHLAND CLAN

LOKI-Book One
TORRIAN-Book Two
LILY-Book Three
JAKE-Book Four
ASHLYN-Book Five
MOLLY-Book Six
JAMIE AND GRACIE-Book Seven
SORCHA-Book Eight
KYLA-Book Nine
BETHIA-Book Ten
LOKI'S CHRISTMAS STORY-Book Eleven
ELIZABETH-Book Twelve

THE BAND OF COUSINS

HIGHLAND VENGEANCE
HIGHLAND ABDUCTION
HIGHLAND RETRIBUTION
HIGHLAND LIES
HIGHLAND FORTITUDE
HIGHLAND RESILIENCE
HIGHLAND DEVOTION
HIGHLAND BRAWN
HIGHLAND YULETIDE MAGIC

HIGHLAND SWORDS

THE SCOT'S BETRAYAL
THE SCOT'S SPY
THE SCOT'S PURSUIT
THE SCOT'S QUEST
THE SCOT'S DECEPTION
THE SCOT'S ANGEL

THE SOULMATE CHRONICLES TRILOGY

#1 TRUSTING A HIGHLANDER
#2 TRUSTING A SCOT
#3 TRUSTING A CHIEFTAIN

STAND-ALONE BOOKS

ESCAPE TO THE HIGHLANDS
THE BANISHED HIGHLANDER
REFORMING THE DUKE-REGENCY
WOLF AND THE WILD SCOTS
FALLING FOR THE CHIEFTAIN-3RD in a collaborative trilogy
HIGHLAND SECRETS -3rd in a collaborative trilogy

THE SUMMERHILL SERIES-CONTEMPORARY ROMANCE

#1-ONE SUMMERHILL DAY
#2-A FRESH START FOR TWO
#3-THREE REASONS TO LOVE

ABOUT THE AUTHOR

Keira Montclair is the pen name of an author who lives in South Carolina with her husband. She loves to write fast-paced, emotional romance, especially with children as secondary characters.

When she's not writing, she loves to spend time with her grandchildren. She's worked as a high school math teacher, a registered nurse, and an office manager. She loves ballet, mathematics, puzzles, learning anything new, and creating new characters for her readers to fall in love with.

She writes historical romantic suspense. Her best-selling series is a family saga that follows two medieval Scottish clans through four generations and now numbers over thirty books.

Contact her through her website:
keiramontclair.com.

Printed in Great Britain
by Amazon